Russian Fairy Tales

Recorded by
Alexander Afanasyev

Illustrations by
Ivan Bilibin

Russian Fairy Tales by Alexander Afanasyev
Illustrations by Ivan Bilibin
Translation by Post Wheeler

ISBN 978-1-916581-17-3
Published by The Planet, 2023
© The Planet, 2023: book design
www.the-planet-books.com

Contents

Vasilisa the Beautiful..................5

Maria Morevna..................22

The Feather of Finist the Falcon..................38

The Frog-Tsarevna..................51

Tsarevich Ivan,
the Firebird and the Grey..................64

Vasilisa the Beautiful

In a certain Tsardom, across three times nine kingdoms, beyond high mountain chains, there once lived a merchant. He had been married for twelve years, but in that time there had been born to him only one child, a daughter, who from her cradle was called Vasilisa the Beautiful. When the little girl was eight years old, her mother fell ill, and before many days it was plain to be seen that she must die. So she called her little daughter to her, took a tiny wooden doll from under the blanket of the bed, put it into her hands and said: "My little Vasilisa, my dear daughter, listen to what I say, remember well my last words and fail not to carry out my wishes. I am dying, and with my blessing, I leave to thee this little doll. It is very precious, for there is no other like it in the whole world. Carry it always about with thee in thy pocket and never show it to anyone. When evil threatens thee or sorrow befalls thee, go into a corner, take it from thy pocket and give it something to eat and drink. It will eat and drink a little, and then thou mayest tell it thy trouble and ask its advice, and it will tell thee how to act in thy time of need." So saying, she kissed her little daughter on the forehead, blessed her, and shortly after died.

Little Vasilisa grieved greatly for her mother, and her sorrow was so deep that when the dark night came, she lay in her bed and wept and did not sleep. At length she bethought herself of the tiny doll, so she rose and took it from the pocket of her gown, and finding a piece of wheat bread and a cup of kvass, she set them before it and said: "There, my little doll, take it. Eat a little, and drink a little, and listen to my grief. My dear mother is dead, and I am lonely for her."

Then the doll's eyes began to shine like fireflies, and suddenly it became alive. It ate a morsel of the bread and took a sip of the kvass, and when it had eaten and drank, it said: "Don't weep, little Vasilisa. Grief is worst at night. Lie down, shut thine eyes, comfort thyself and go to sleep. The morning is wiser than the evening." So Vasilisa the Beautiful lay down, comforted herself and went to sleep, and the next day her grieving was not so deep and her tears were less bitter.

Now after the death of his wife, the merchant sorrowed for many days as was right, but at the end of that time he began to desire to marry again and to look about him for a suitable wife. This was not difficult to find, for he had a fine house with a stable of swift horses, besides being a good man who gave much to the poor. Of all the women he saw, however, the one who, to his mind, suited him best of all, was a widow of about his own age with two daughters of her own, and she, he thought, besides being a good housekeeper, would be a kind foster mother to his little Vasilisa.

So the merchant married the widow and brought her home as his wife, but the little girl soon found that her foster mother was very far from being what her father had thought. She was a cold, cruel woman, who had desired the merchant for the sake of his wealth, and had no love for his daughter. Vasilisa was the greatest beauty in the whole village, while the daughters of the foster mother were as spare and homely as two crows, and because of this all three envied and hated Vasilisa. They gave her all sorts of errands to run and difficult tasks to perform, in order that the toil might make her thin and worn, and that her face might grow brown from sun and wind; and they treated her so cruelly as to leave few joys in life for her. But little Vasilisa endured all this without complaint, and while the stepmother's two daughters grew always thinner and uglier in spite of the fact that they had no hard tasks to do, never went out in cold or rain, and sat always with their arms folded like ladies of a Court, she herself had cheeks like blood and milk and grew every day more and more beautiful.

Now the reason for this was the tiny doll, without whose help little Vasilisa could never have managed to do all the work that was laid upon her. Each night, when everyone else was sound asleep, she would get up from her bed, take the doll into a closet, and locking the door, give it something to eat and drink, and say: "There, my little doll, take it. Eat a little, drink a little, and listen to my grief. I live in my father's house, but my spiteful stepmother wishes to drive me out of the white world. Tell me! How shall I act, and what shall I do?"

Then the little doll's eyes would begin to shine like glowworms, and it would become alive. It would eat a little food and sip a little drink, and then it would comfort her and tell her how to act. While Vasilisa slept, it would get ready all her work for the next day, so that she had only to rest in the shade and gather flowers, for the doll would have the kitchen garden weeded, and the beds of cabbage watered, and plenty of fresh water brought from the well, and the stoves heated exactly right. And, besides this, the little doll told her how to make, from a certain herb, an ointment which prevented her from ever being sunburnt. So all the joy in life that came to Vasilisa came to her through the tiny doll that she always carried in her pocket.

Years passed, till Vasilisa grew up and became of an age when it is good to marry. All the young men in the village, high and low, rich and poor, asked for her hand, while not one of them stopped even to look at the stepmother's two daughters, so ill-favoured were they. This angered their mother still more against Vasilisa; she answered every gallant who came with the same words: "Never shall the younger be wed before the older ones!" and each time, when she had let a suitor out of the door, she would soothe her anger and hatred by beating her stepdaughter. So while Vasilisa grew each day more lovely and graceful, she was often miserable, and but for the little doll in her pocket, would have longed to leave the white world.

Now there came a time when it became necessary for the merchant to leave his home and to travel to a distant Tsardom. He bade farewell to his wife and her two daughters, kissed Vasilisa and gave her his blessing and departed, bidding them say a prayer each day for his safe return. Scarce was he out of sight of the village, however, when his wife sold his house, packed all his goods and moved with them to another dwelling far from the town, in a gloomy neighbourhood on the edge of a wild forest. Here, every day, while her two daughters were working indoors, the merchant's wife would send Vasilisa on one errand or other into the forest, either to find a branch of a certain rare bush or to bring her flowers or berries.

Now deep in this forest, as the stepmother well knew, there was a green lawn, and on the lawn stood a little hut on hens' legs, where lived a certain Baba Yaga, an old witch grandmother. She lived alone, and none dared go near the hut, for she ate people as one eats chickens. The merchant's wife sent Vasilisa into the forest each day, hoping she might meet the old witch and be devoured; but always the girl came home safe and sound, because the little doll showed her where the bush, the flowers and the berries grew, and did not let her go near the hut that stood on hens' legs. And each time the stepmother hated her more and more because she came to no harm.

One autumn evening the merchant's wife called the three girls to her and gave them each a task. One of her daughters she bade make a piece of lace, the other to knit a pair of hose, and to Vasilisa she gave a basket of flax to be spun. She bade each finish a certain amount. Then she put out all the fires in the house, leaving only a single candle lighted in the room where the three girls worked, and she herself went to sleep.

They worked an hour, they worked two hours, they worked three hours, when one of the elder daughters took up the tongs to straighten the wick of the candle. She pretended to do this awkwardly (as her mother had bidden her) and put the candle out, as if by accident.

"What are we to do now?" asked her sister. "The fires are all out, there is no other light in all the house, and our tasks are not done."

"We must go and fetch fire," said the first. "The only house near is a hut in the forest, where a Baba Yaga lives. One of us must go and borrow fire from her."

"I have enough light from my steel pins," said the one who was making the lace, "and I will not go."

"And I have plenty of light from my silver needles," said the other, who was knitting the hose, "and I will not go."

"Thou, Vasilisa," they both said, "shalt go and fetch the fire, for thou hast neither steel pins nor silver needles and cannot see to spin thy flax!" They both rose up, pushed Vasilisa out of the house and locked the door, crying: "Thou shalt not come in till thou hast fetched the fire."

Vasilisa sat down on the doorstep, took the tiny doll from one pocket and from another the supper she had ready for it, put the food before it and said: "There, my little doll, take it. Eat a little and listen to my sorrow. I must go to the hut of the old Baba Yaga in the dark forest to borrow some fire, and I fear she will eat me. Tell me! What shall I do?"

Then the doll's eyes began to shine like two stars, and it became alive. It ate a little and said: "Do not fear, little Vasilisa. Go where thou hast been sent. While I am with thee, no harm shall come to thee from the old witch." So Vasilisa put the doll back into her pocket, crossed herself and started out into the dark, wild forest.

Whether she walked a short way or a long way, the telling is easy, but the journey was hard. The wood was very dark, and she could not help trembling from fear. Suddenly she heard the sound of a horse's hoofs, and a man on horseback galloped past her. He was dressed all in white, the horse under him was milk-white, and the harness was white; and just as he passed her, it became twilight.

She went a little further, and again she heard the sound of a horse's hoofs, and there came another man on horseback galloping past her. He was dressed all in red, and

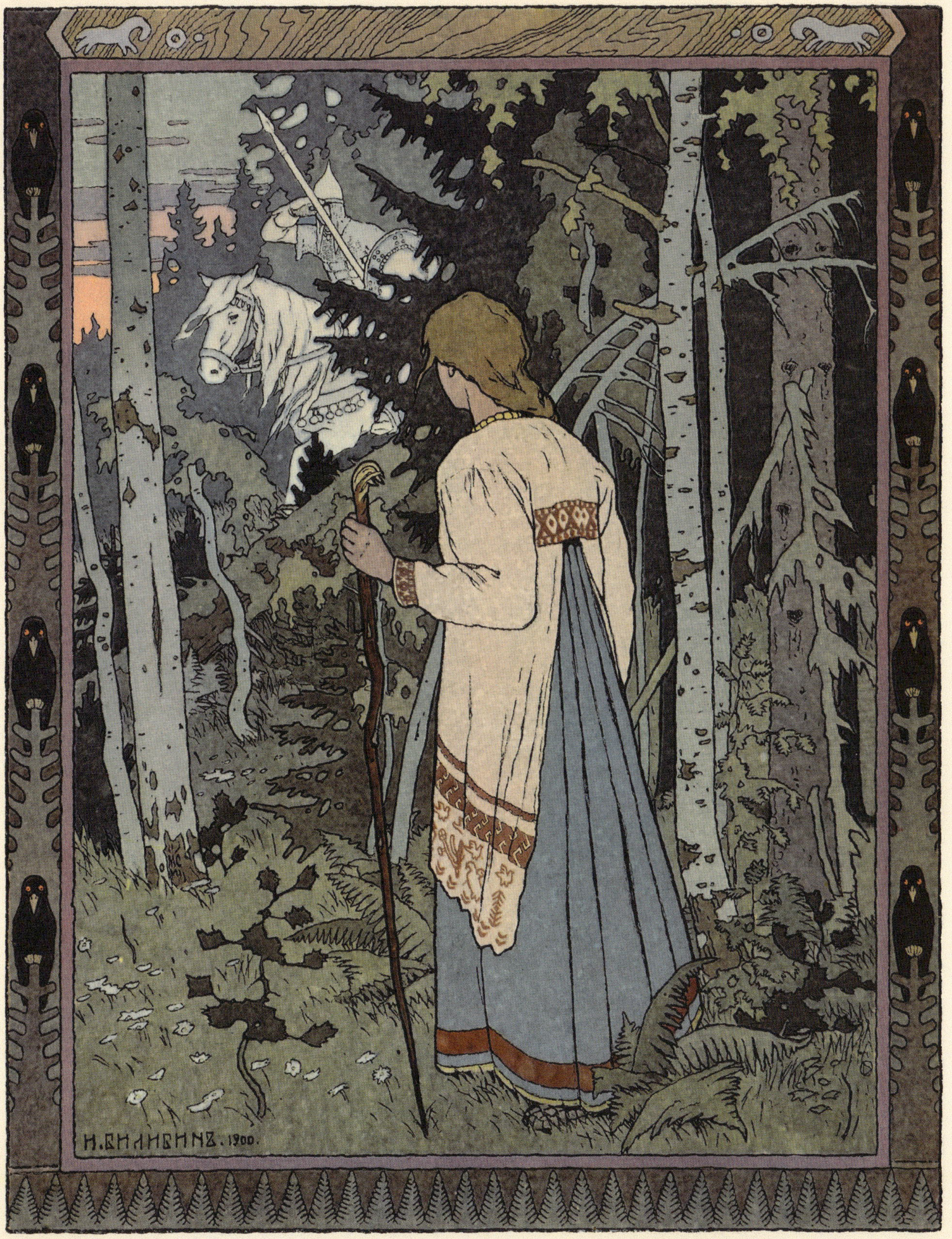
И.БИЛИБИНЪ.1900.

the horse under him was blood-red, and its harness was red; and just as he passed her, the sun rose.

That whole day Vasilisa walked, for she had lost her way. She could find no path at all in the dark wood, and she had no food to set before the little doll to make it alive.

But at evening she came all at once to the green lawn where the wretched little hut stood on its hens' legs. The wall around the hut was made of human bones, and on its top were skulls. There was a gate in the wall, whose hinges were the bones of human feet and whose locks were jaw bones set with sharp teeth. The sight filled Vasilisa with horror, and she stopped as still as a post buried in the ground.

As she stood there, a third man on horseback came galloping up. His face was black, he was dressed all in black, and the horse he rode was coal-black. He galloped up to the gate of the hut and disappeared there as if he had sunk through the ground; and at that moment the night came, and the forest grew dark.

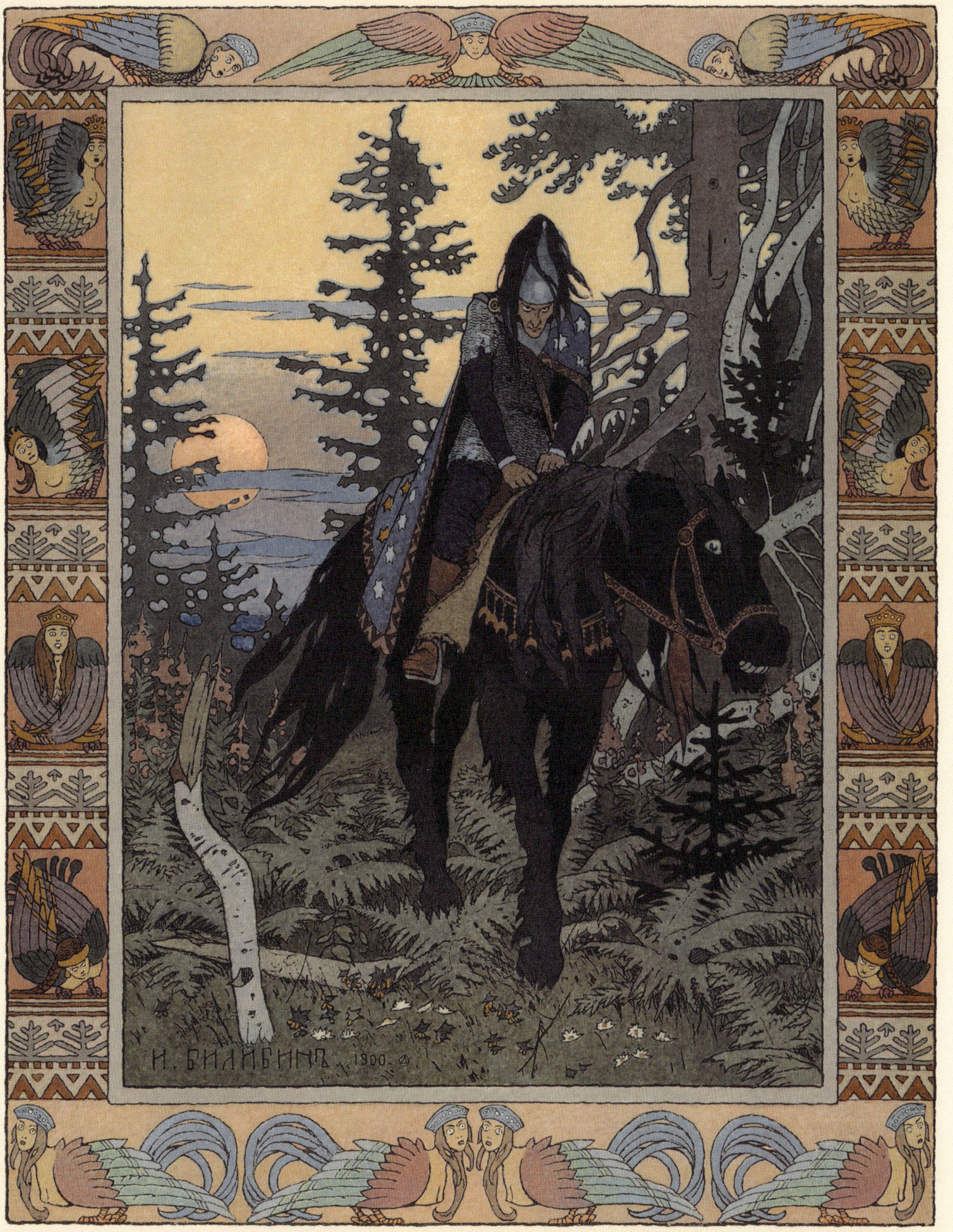
И. БИЛИБИНЪ
1900.

But it was not dark on the green lawn, for instantly the eyes of all the skulls on the wall were lighted up and shone till the place was as bright as day. Seeing this, Vasilisa trembled with fear so that she could not run away.

Then suddenly the wood became full of a terrible noise; the trees began to groan, the branches to creak and the dry leaves to rustle; and the Baba Yaga came flying from the forest. She was riding in a great iron mortar and driving it with a pestle; and she swept away the trail behind her with a kitchen broom.

She rode up to the gate and, stopping, said:

> "Little Hut, little Hut,
> "Stand the way thy mother placed thee,
> "Turn thy back to the forest and thy face to me!"

And the little hut turned facing her and stood still. Then smelling all around her, she cried: "Foo! Foo! I smell a smell that is Russian. Who is here?"

Vasilisa, in great fright, came nearer to the old woman and, bowing very low, said: "It is only Vasilisa, grandmother. My stepmother's daughters sent me to thee to borrow some fire."

"Well," said the old witch, "I know them. But if I give thee the fire, thou shalt stay with me some time and do some work to pay for it. If not, thou shalt be eaten for my supper." Then she turned to the gate and shouted: "Ho! ye, my solid locks, unlock! Thou, my stout gate, open!" Instantly the locks unlocked, the gate opened of itself, and the Baba Yaga rode in whistling. Vasilisa entered behind her, and immediately the gate shut again and the locks snapped tight.

When they had entered the hut, the old witch threw herself down on the stove, stretched out her bony legs and said: "Come, fetch and put on the table at once everything that is in the oven. I am hungry." So Vasilisa ran and lighted a splinter of wood from one of the skulls on the wall and took the food from the oven and set it before her. There was enough cooked meat for three strong men. She brought also from the cellar kvass, honey, beer and wine; and the Baba Yaga ate and drank the whole, leaving the girl only a little of cabbage soup, a crust of bread and a morsel of sucking pig.

When her hunger was satisfied, the old witch, growing drowsy, lay down on the stove and said: "Listen to me well and do what I bid thee. Tomorrow when I drive away, do thou clean the yard, sweep the floors and cook my supper. Then take a quarter of a measure of wheat from my storehouse and pick out of it all the black grains and the wild peas. Mind thou dost all that I have bade; if not, thou shalt be eaten for my supper."

Presently the Baba Yaga turned toward the wall and began to snore, and Vasilisa knew that she was fast asleep. Then she went into the corner, took the tiny doll from her pocket, put before it a bit of bread and a little cabbage soup that she had saved, burst into tears and said: "There, my little doll, take it. Eat a little, drink a little, and listen to my grief. Here I am in the house of the old witch, and the gate in the wall is locked, and I am afraid. She has given me a difficult task, and if I do not do all she has bade, she will eat me tomorrow. Tell me: what shall I do?"

Then the eyes of the little doll began to shine like two candles. It ate a little of the bread and drank a little of the soup and said: "Don't be afraid, Vasilisa the Beautiful. Be comforted. Say thy prayers and go to sleep. The morning is wiser than the evening." So Vasilisa trusted the little doll and was comforted. She said her prayers, lay down on the floor and went fast asleep.

When she woke next morning, very early, it was still dark. She rose and looked out of the window, and she saw that the eyes of the skulls on the wall were growing dim. As she looked, the man dressed all in white, riding the milk-white horse, galloped swiftly around the corner of the hut, leaped the wall and disappeared; and as he went, it became quite light and the eyes of the skulls flickered and went out. The old witch was in the yard; now she began to whistle, and the great iron mortar and pestle and the kitchen broom flew out of the hut to her. As she got into the mortar, the man dressed all in red mounted on the blood-red horse, galloped like the wind around the corner of the hut, leaped the wall and was gone; and at that moment the sun rose. Then the Baba Yaga shouted: "Ho! ye, my solid locks, unlock! Thou, my stout gate, open!" The locks unlocked and the gate opened, and she rode away in the mortar, driving with the pestle and sweeping away the trail behind her with the broom.

When Vasilisa found herself left alone, she examined the hut, wondering to find it filled with such an abundance of everything. Then she stood still, remembering all the work that she had been bidden to do and wondering what to begin first. But as she looked, she rubbed her eyes: the yard was already neatly cleaned and the floors were nicely swept, and the little doll was sitting in the storehouse picking the last black grains and wild peas out of the quarter measure of wheat.

Vasilisa ran and took the little doll in her arms. "My dearest little doll!" she cried. "Thou hast saved me from my trouble! Now I have only to cook the Baba Yaga's supper, since all the rest of the tasks are done!"

"Cook it, with God's help," said the doll, "and then rest, and may the cooking of it make you healthy!" And so saying it crept into her pocket and became again only a little wooden doll.

So Vasilisa rested all day and was refreshed; and when it grew toward evening, she laid the table for the old witch's supper and sat looking out of the window, waiting for her coming. After awhile she heard the sound of horse's hoofs, and the man in black, on the coal-black horse, galloped up to the wall gate and disappeared like a great dark shadow; and instantly it became quite dark, and the eyes of all the skulls began to glitter and shine.

Then all at once the trees of the forest began to creak and groan, and the leaves and the bushes to moan and sigh; and the Baba Yaga came riding out of the dark wood in the huge iron mortar, driving with the pestle and sweeping out the trail behind her with the kitchen broom. Vasilisa let her in, and the witch, smelling all around her, asked:

"Well, hast thou done perfectly all the tasks I gave thee to do, or am I to eat thee for my supper?"

"Be so good as to look for thyself, grandmother," answered Vasilisa.

The Baba Yaga went all about the place, tapping with her iron pestle, and carefully examining everything. But so well had the little doll done its work that, try as hard as she might, the old witch could not find anything to complain of. There was not a weed left in the yard, nor a speck of dust on the floors, nor a single black grain or wild pea in the wheat.

She was greatly angered, but was obliged to pretend to be pleased. "Well," she said, "thou hast done all well." Then, clapping her hands, she shouted: "Ho! my faithful servants! Friends of my heart! Haste and grind my wheat!" Immediately three pairs of hands appeared, seized the measure of wheat and carried it away.

The Baba Yaga sat down to supper, and Vasilisa put before her all the food from the oven, with kvass, honey, beer and wine. The old witch ate it, bones and all, almost to the last morsel, enough for four strong men, and then, growing drowsy, stretched her bony legs on the stove and said: "Tomorrow do as thou hast done today, and besides these tasks take from my storehouse a half-measure of poppy seeds and clean them one by one. Someone has mixed earth with them to do me a mischief and to anger me, and I will have them made perfectly clean." So saying she turned to the wall and soon began to snore.

When she was fast asleep, Vasilisa went into the corner, took the little doll from her pocket, set before it a part of the food that was left and asked its advice. And the doll, when it had become alive and eaten a little food and sipped a little drink, said: "Don't worry, beautiful Vasilisa! Be comforted. Do as thou didst last night: say thy prayers and go to sleep." So Vasilisa was comforted. She said her prayers and went to sleep and did not wake till next morning when she heard the old witch in the yard

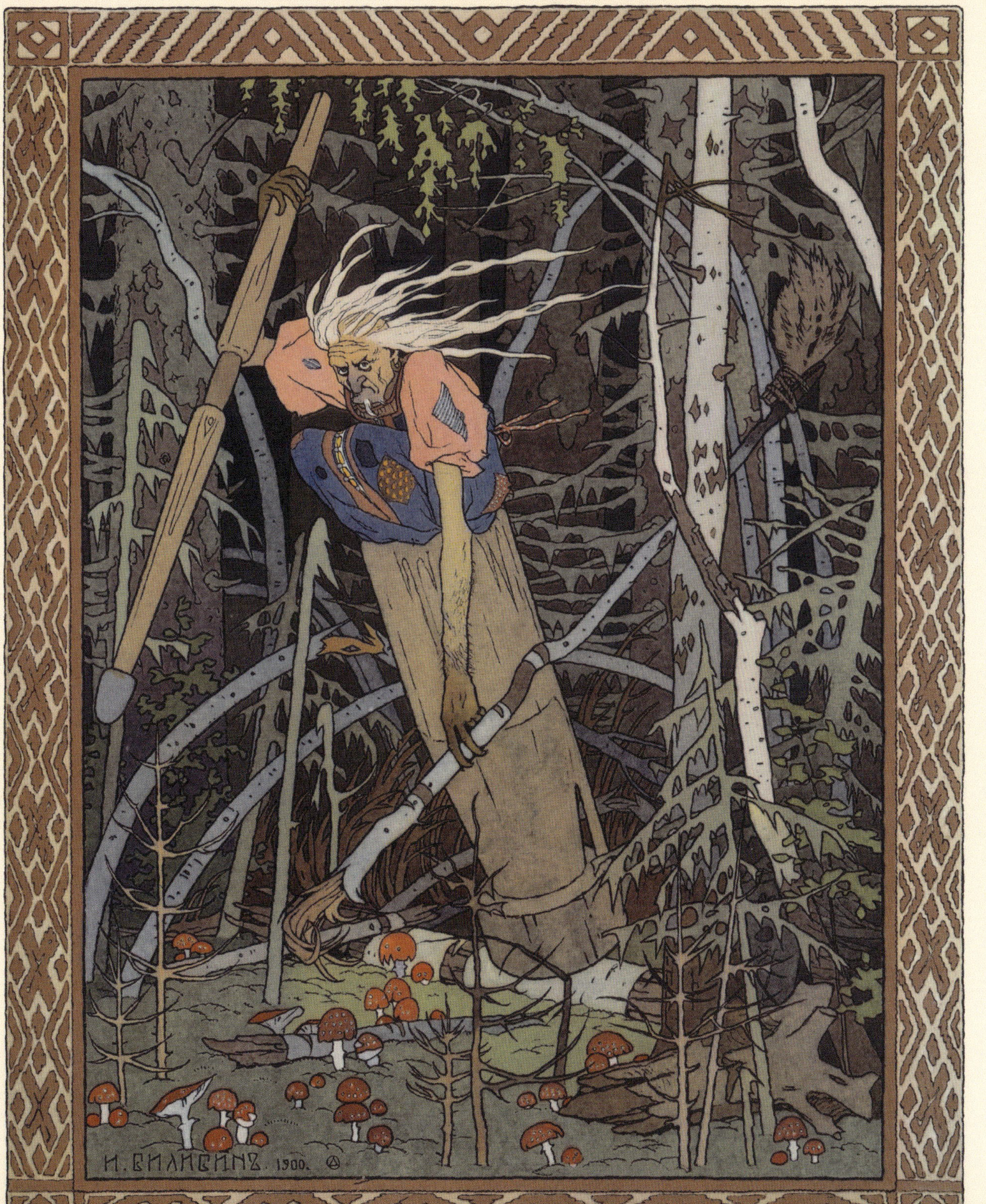
И. БИЛИБИНЪ. 1900.

whistling. She ran to the window just in time to see her take her place in the big iron mortar; and as she did so, the man dressed all in red, riding on the blood-red horse, leaped over the wall and was gone, just as the sun rose over the wild forest.

As it had happened on the first morning, so it happened now. When Vasilisa looked, she found that the little doll had finished all the tasks except the cooking of the supper. The yard was swept and in order, the floors were as clean as new wood, and there was not a grain of earth left in the half-measure of poppy seeds. She rested and refreshed herself till the afternoon when she cooked the supper; and when evening came, she laid the table and sat down to wait for the old witch's coming.

Soon the man in black, on the coal-black horse, galloped up to the gate, and the dark fell, and the eyes of the skulls began to shine like day; then the ground began to quake, and the trees of the forest began to creak, and the dry leaves to rustle, and the Baba Yaga came riding in her iron mortar, driving with her pestle and sweeping away her trail with her broom.

When she came in, she smelled around her and went all about the hut, tapping with the pestle; but pry and examine as she might, again she could see no reason to find fault and was angrier than ever.

She clapped her hands and shouted: "Ho! my trusty servants! Friends of my soul! Haste and press the oil out of my poppy seeds!"

And instantly the three pairs of hands appeared, seized the measure of poppy seeds and carried it away.

Presently the old witch sat down to supper, and Vasilisa brought all she had cooked, enough for five grown men, and set it before her, and brought beer and honey; and then she herself stood silently waiting. The Baba Yaga ate and drank it all, every morsel, leaving not so much as a crumb of bread; then she said snappishly: "Well, why dost thou say nothing, but stand there as if thou wast dumb?"

"I spoke not," Vasilisa answered, "because I dared not. But if thou wilt allow me, grandmother, I wish to ask thee some questions."

"Well," said the old witch, "only remember that every question does not lead to good. If thou knowest overmuch, thou wilt grow old too soon. What wilt thou ask?"

"I would ask thee," said Vasilisa, "of the men on horseback. When I came to thy hut, a rider passed me. He was dressed all in white, and he rode a milk-white horse. Who was he?"

"That was my white, bright day," answered the Baba Yaga angrily. "He is a servant of mine, but he cannot hurt thee. Ask me more."

"Afterwards," said Vasilisa, "a second rider overtook me. He was dressed in red, and the horse he rode was blood-red. Who was he?"

"That was my servant, the round, red sun," answered the Baba Yaga, "and he, too, cannot injure thee," and she ground her teeth. "Ask me more."

"A third rider," said Vasilisa, "came galloping up to the gate. He was black, his clothes were black, and the horse was coal-black. Who was he?"

"That was my servant, the black, dark night," answered the old witch furiously; "but he also cannot harm thee. Ask me more."

But Vasilisa, remembering what the Baba Yaga had said, that not every question led to good, was silent.

"Ask me more!" cried the old witch. "Why dost thou not ask me more? Ask me of the three pairs of hands that serve me!"

But Vasilisa saw how she snarled at her and she answered: "The three questions are enough for me. As thou hast said, grandmother, I would not, through knowing over much, become too soon old."

"It is well for thee," said the Baba Yaga, "that thou didst not ask of them, but only of what thou didst see outside of this hut. Hadst thou asked of them, my servants, the three pairs of hands would have seized thee also, as they did the wheat and poppy seeds, to be my food. Now I would ask a question in my turn: How is it that thou hast been able, in a little time, to do perfectly all the tasks I gave thee? Tell me!"

Vasilisa was so frightened to see how the old witch ground her teeth that she almost told her of the little doll; but she bethought herself just in time and answered: "The blessing of my dead mother helps me."

Then the Baba Yaga sprang up in a fury. "Get thee out of my house this moment!" she shrieked. "I want no one who bears a blessing to cross my threshold! Get thee gone!"

Vasilisa ran to the yard, and behind her she heard the old witch shouting to the locks and the gate. The locks opened, the gate swung wide, and she ran out on to the lawn. The Baba Yaga seized from the wall one of the skulls with burning eyes and flung it after her. "There," she howled, "is the fire for thy stepmother's daughters. Take it. That is what they sent thee here for, and may they have joy of it!"

Vasilisa put the skull on the end of a stick and darted away through the forest, running as fast as she could, finding her path by the skull's glowing eyes, which went out only when morning came.

Whether she ran a long way or a short way, and whether the road was smooth or rough, towards evening of the next day, when the eyes in the skull were beginning to glimmer, she came out of the dark, wild forest to her stepmother's house.

When she came near to the gate, she thought, "Surely, by this time they will have found some fire," and threw the skull into the hedge; but it spoke to her and

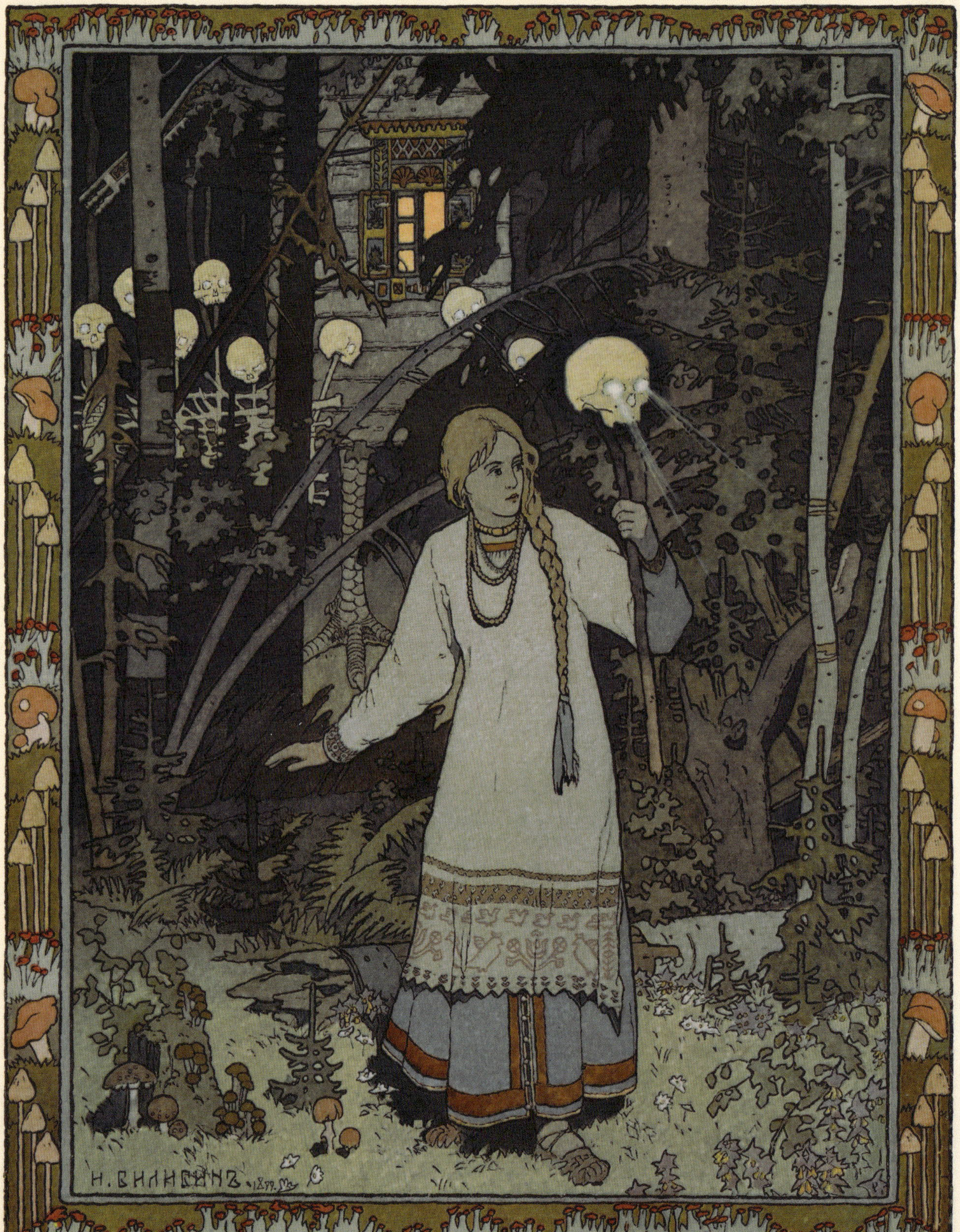
И. БИЛИБИНЪ
1899

said: "Do not throw me away, beautiful Vasilisa; bring me to thy stepmother." So, looking at the house and seeing no spark of light in any of the windows, she took up the skull again and carried it with her.

Now since Vasilisa had gone, the stepmother and her two daughters had had neither fire nor light in all the house. When they struck flint and steel, the tinder would not catch, and the fire they brought from the neighbours would go out immediately as soon as they carried it over the threshold, so that they had been unable to light or warm themselves or to cook food to eat. Therefore now, for the first time in her life, Vasilisa found herself welcomed. They opened the door to her, and the merchant's wife was greatly rejoiced to find that the light in the skull did not go out as soon as it was brought in. "Maybe the witch's fire will stay," she said, took the skull into the best room, set it on a candlestick and called her two daughters to admire it.

But the eyes of the skull suddenly began to glimmer and to glow like red coals, and wherever the three turned or ran, the eyes followed them, growing larger and brighter till they flamed like two furnaces, and hotter and hotter till the merchant's wife and her two wicked daughters took fire and were burned to ashes. Only Vasilisa the Beautiful was not touched.

In the morning Vasilisa dug a deep hole in the ground and buried the skull. Then she locked the house and set out to the village, where she went to live with an old woman who was poor and childless; and so she remained for many days, waiting for her father's return from the far-distant kingdom.

But, sitting lonely, time soon began to hang heavy on her hands. One day she said to the old woman: "It is dull for me, grandmother, to sit idly hour by hour. My hands want work to do. Go, therefore, and buy me some flax, the best and finest to be found anywhere, and at least I can spin."

The old woman hastened and bought some flax of the best sort, and Vasilisa sat down to work. So well did she spin that the thread came out as even and fine as a hair, and presently there was enough to begin to weave. But so fine was the thread that no frame could be found to weave it upon, nor would any weaver undertake to make one.

Then Vasilisa went into her closet, took the little doll from her pocket, set food and drink before it and asked its help. And after it had eaten a little and drunk a little, the doll became alive and said: "Bring me an old frame and an old basket and some hairs from a horse's mane, and I will arrange everything for thee." Vasilisa hastened to fetch all the doll had asked for, and when evening came, she said her prayers, went to sleep, and in the morning she found ready a frame, perfectly made, to weave her fine thread upon.

She wove one month, she wove two months—all the winter Vasilisa sat weaving, weaving her fine thread, till the whole piece of linen was done, of a texture so fine that it could be passed, like thread, through the eye of a needle. When the spring came, she bleached it, so white that no snow could be compared with it. Then she said to the old woman: "Take thou the linen to the market, grandmother, and sell it, and the money shall suffice to pay for my food and lodging." When the old woman had examined the linen, however, she said: "Never will I sell such cloth in the marketplace; no one should wear it except it be the Tsar himself, and tomorrow I shall carry it to the Palace."

Next day, accordingly, the old woman went to the Tsar's splendid Palace and fell to walking up and down before the windows. The servants came to ask her her errand but she answered them nothing, and kept walking up and down. At length the Tsar opened his window and asked: "What dost thou want, old woman, that thou walkest here?"

"O Tsar's Majesty!" the old woman answered, "I have with me a marvellous piece of linen stuff, so wondrously woven that I will show it to none but thee."

The Tsar bade them bring her before him, and when he saw the linen, he was struck with astonishment at its fineness and beauty. "What wilt thou take for it, old woman?" he asked.

"There is no price that can buy it, our Father Tsar," she answered; "but I have brought it to thee as a gift." The Tsar could not thank the old woman enough. He took the linen and sent her to her house with many rich presents.

Seamstresses were called to make shirts for him out of the cloth; but when it had been cut up, so fine was it that no one of them was deft and skillful enough to sew it. The best seamstresses in all the Tsardom were summoned but none dared undertake it. So at last the Tsar sent for the old woman and said: "If thou didst know how to spin such thread and weave such linen, thou must also know how to sew me shirts from it."

And the old woman answered: "O Tsar's Majesty, it was not I who wove the linen; it is the work of my adopted daughter."

"Take it, then," the Tsar said, "and bid her do it for me."

The old woman brought the linen home and told Vasilisa the Tsar's command: "Well, I knew that the work would needs be done by my own hands," said Vasilisa, and, locking herself in her own room, began to make the shirts. So fast and well did she work that soon a dozen were ready. Then the old woman carried them to the Tsar, while Vasilisa washed her face, dressed her hair, put on her best gown and sat down at the window to see what would happen. And presently a servant in the livery of the Palace came to the house and said: "The Tsar, our lord, desires himself to see the clever needlewoman who has made his shirts and to reward her with his own hands."

Vasilisa rose and went at once to the Palace, and as soon as the Tsar saw her, he fell in love with her with all his soul. He took her by her white hand and made her sit beside him. "Beautiful maiden," he said, "never will I part from thee, and thou shalt be my wife."

So the Tsar and Vasilisa the Beautiful were married, and her father returned from the far distant kingdom, and he and the old woman lived always with her in the splendid Palace, in all joy and contentment. And as for the little wooden doll, Vasilisa carried it about with her in her pocket all her life long.

Maria Morevna

Far behind the blue sea-ocean, beyond the void places, in a city set in the midst of pleasant meads, there lived a Tsarevich whose name was Alexis, and he had three sisters: Tsarevna Anna, Tsarevna Olga and Tsarevna Helena. Their mother had long been dead; and when it came the father's time to die, he called the Tsarevich to him and put the three sisters in his care.

"Heed thou, my dear son, my counsel and command," he said. "Keep not thy sisters overlong with thee, nor delay their marriage, but whoever may be first to ask the hand of either of them, to that one, if she consent, give her to be wed."

So the father died and was buried, and the Tsarevich and his sisters sorrowed, as was right, until time had dulled their grief. Before the Palace there was a fenced garden, where, in the cool of the day, they used to walk together; and often, as they walked, the Tsarevnas would recall their father's words and would say one to another: "I wonder which will be the first to be wed and what manner of lover will come wooing her."

One day as they strolled under the green trees, plucking red poppies, a great cloud, black as ink and shaped like a hawk, suddenly rose in the sky. "Let us hasten indoors, little sisters," said Tsarevich Alexis, "for a dreadful storm is about to break." They quickened their steps, and just as they entered the Palace, a crash of thunder sounded, the roof split in two and a bright hawk came flying in. It alighted on the floor and was instantly transformed into a handsome youth.

"Greeting to thee, Tsarevich Alexis!" said the youth. "Once I came to thy land as a visitor, but now I come as a suitor. I pray thee give me to wife thy sister Anna."

"If she choose to wed thee, I shall not forbid," answered the Tsarevich. "How sayest thou, my sister?"

So comely was the youth that Tsarevna Anna at once agreed, and the same day they were married and set out for the Hawk's Tsardom.

Hours grew into days, and days ran swiftly after one another till a year had vanished as if it had never been. Again one day Tsarevich Alexis went walking with his two sisters in the green garden, and again there rose up in the sky a cloud like a huge black eagle, with white lightnings flashing across it. "Let us seek shelter, little sisters," he said, "for a terrible whirlwind is rising." They hurried to the Palace, and as they entered it, the thunder roared, the ceiling split in two and into the gap came flying an eagle. It alighted on the floor and instantly turned into a comely youth.

"Health to thee, Tsarevich Alexis!" he said. "Heretofore I came to thy Tsardom as a visitor, but now I come to woo. Give me, I beseech thee, thy sister Olga for my wife."

"If she so wills, then will I not deny thee," replied the Tsarevich. "What is thy mind, my sister?"

The Hawk had been well-favoured, but the Eagle was more handsome, and Tsarevna Olga lost no time in accepting him; the same day the marriage was performed, and the Eagle took her away to his own country.

Another year passed swiftly, and one day the Tsarevich said: "Come, little sister, let us walk in the green garden and refresh ourselves." As they strolled among its flowers, again there rose a cloud shaped like a great black crow, and the Tsarevich said: "Let us return with all speed to the Palace, for a fierce tornado is upon us." They did so, but before they had had time to sit down, there came a terrific clap of thunder, the ceiling split and opened, and into the room flew a crow. As it alighted, it became a graceful youth, who said:

"Prosperity to thee, Tsarevich Alexis! In the past I came to thy realm as a visitor, but now I come seeking a wife. Grant me, I pray, thy sister Helena to wed."

"If she favour thy suit, I may not refuse her," returned the Tsarevich. "Wilt thou say 'aye,' my sister?"

The Hawk and the Eagle had been handsome, but the Crow was even more brilliant and splendid than they, and Tsarevna Helena agreed without delay. The marriage took place at once, and the Crow set out with his bride for his own Tsardom.

Tsarevich Alexis, left solitary, was sad and lonely, and when a whole year had passed without sight or sound of his sisters, he said to himself: "I will go and search for my three little sisters." So he called for his best horse and rode out into the white world.

He rode one day, he rode two days, he rode three days, till he came to a plain whereon a numerous army, with weapons broken and scattered, lay dead and dying. Sitting on his horse, he cried aloud: "If there be one man here left alive, let him answer me. Who hath routed this great host?" And one man whose life was yet in him replied where he lay: "These thousand stout warriors, O Tsarevich, were beaten by Maria Morevna, daughter of three mothers, granddaughter of six grandmothers, sister of nine brothers, the beautiful Tsar's daughter." And saying this he died.

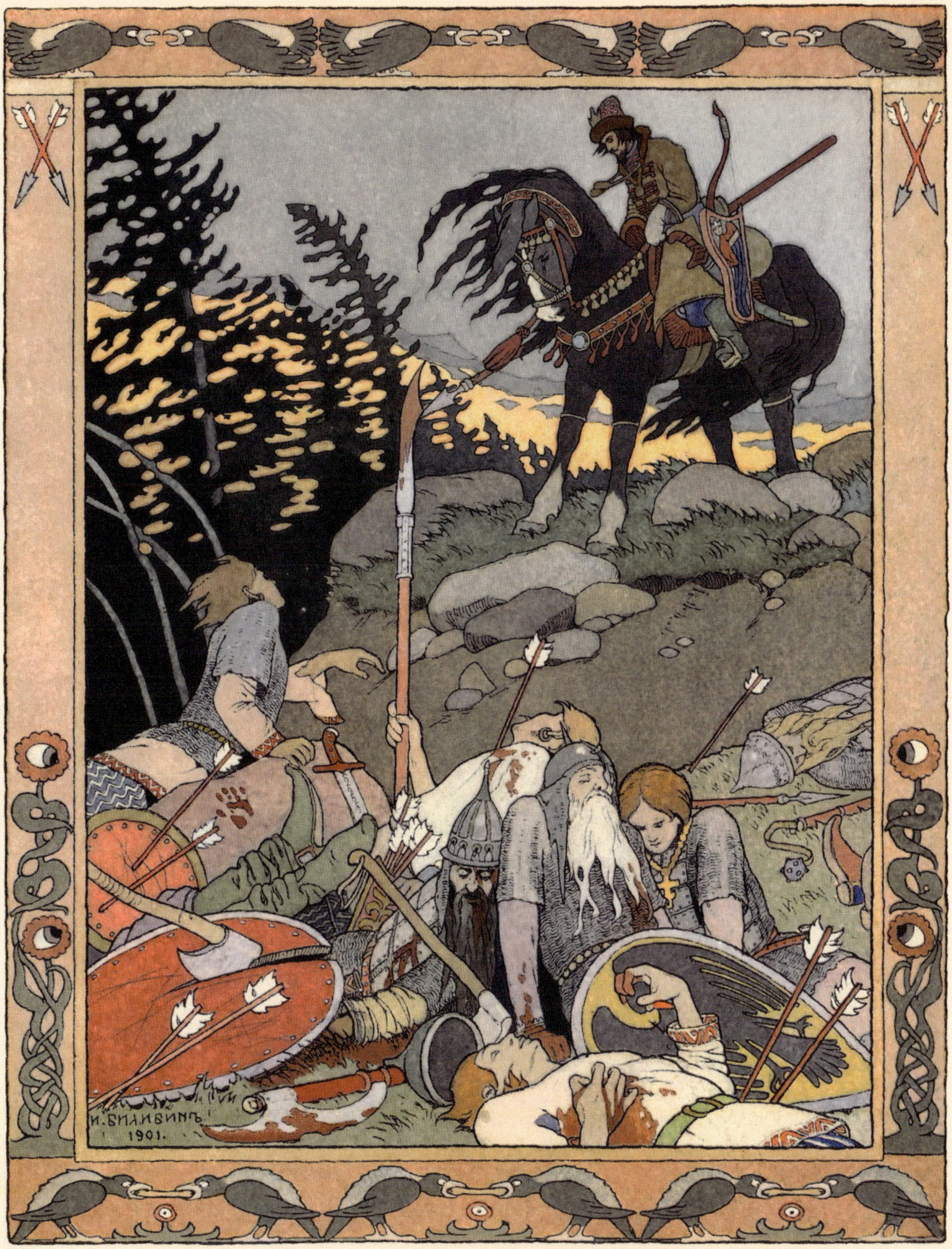
И. БИЛИБИНЪ
1901.

И. Билибинъ. 1900.

Tsarevich Alexis rode on, till at length he came to a multitude of white tents pitched by the way, from the finest of which the lovely Maria Morevna came forth to greet him. "Health to thee, Tsarevich," she said. "Whither dost thou ride? Is it by thine own will or against it?"

Tsarevich Alexis replied: "Brave men, Tsarevna, ride not anywhere against their will."

The beautiful Tsar's daughter was pleased with his answer. "Well," she said, "if thy business be not pressing, I pray thee stay awhile as my guest."

Tsarevich Alexis, nothing loath, dismounted and remained the guest of Maria Morevna; and before two days had passed, they had fallen deeply in love with one another. She took him with her to her maiden Palace, where they were married with great rejoicing, and there they lived many months together in happiness.

Now Maria Morevna was a warrior, and at the end of this time there befell a rebellion on her border; so she called together her army and, leaving Tsarevich Alexis in charge of her Palace, rode to the fight. "Guard and rule all things," she bade him, "only on no account open the door of the locked closet in my inner chamber."

The Tsarevich promised to obey her command, but she had not gone far on her way before his curiosity overmastered him. He went to the inner chamber, unlocked and opened the closet door, and there he saw an old man of huge form hanging from a beam, fettered with twelve riveted iron chains.

"Who art thou?" asked the Tsarevich.

"I am Koschei the Wizard," answered the old man. "Imprisoned by the father of Maria Morevna, I have suffered tortures here for ten years. Have mercy on me, good youth, and fetch me a little water to cool my parched throat!"

The Tsarevich pitied the Wizard. "A drink of water can do no harm," he thought, and went and fetched a jugful. The Wizard took it at a single gulp. "My thirst is too great for a single draught to quench," he said. "I pray thee give me another, and when danger threatens thee I will give thee thy life."

Tsarevich Alexis brought a second jugful, and this also Koschei drank at a draught. "In mercy, give me but one more," he pleaded, "and twice will I give thee thy life when otherwise thou must perish."

The Tsarevich brought him the third jugful, which Koschei also drank at a draught, but as soon as he had swallowed it, all the Wizard's former strength returned; he strained at the twelve chains and broke them asunder like rotten rope. "My thanks to thee, Tsarevich!" he shouted. "Thou art as likely now to possess thy Maria Morevna again as to see thine own ears!" He flew out of the window in a whirlwind, overtook the beautiful Tsar's daughter on her way to the war, seized her from the midst of her army and carried her away across three times nine Tsardoms to his own land.

Tsarevich Alexis, seeing the misfortune his disobedience had wrought, wept bitterly and long. At length he wiped away his tears, and saying to himself, "Whatever may befall, I shall not return until I have found Maria Morevna," he set out across three times nine Tsardoms.

He rode one day, he rode two days, and at dawn on the third day he came to a beautiful Palace of white stone whose roof shone like a rainbow. Before the Palace stood an oak tree, on whose topmost branch perched a Hawk. As soon as it saw him, the Hawk flew down from the tree, alighted on the ground and became a handsome youth. "Welcome, my dear brother-in-law!" he cried. "How hast God dealt with thee these past three years?" The next moment Tsarevna Anna came running from the Palace, and kissing her brother began to ask him many questions and to tell him of what had befallen her.

Tsarevich Alexis spent three days with them, at the end of which time he said: "I can remain no longer, but must go on my search for my wife, Maria Morevna."

His brother-in-law, the Hawk, answered: "It is a far journey. Leave with us thy silver spoon, so that we may look upon it and be reminded of thee."

The Tsarevich left with him the silver spoon and rode on. He rode one day, he rode a second, and on the third, at daybreak, he came to a Palace of grey marble even finer than the Hawk's, whose roof was mother-of-pearl. Before it grew a fir tree and on the tree perched an Eagle, which as soon as it saw the Tsarevich, flew down, alighted, and became a comely young man. "Hasten, wife," cried the Eagle, "our dear brother is coming!" And Tsarevna Olga came running from the Palace, kissed and embraced her brother and began to ply him with questions.

A second three days Tsarevich Alexis spent with them and then said: "Farewell, my dear sister and brother-in-law, I go now to search for my wife, the beautiful Tsar's daughter."

"It is many versts to the Castle of Koschei," said the Eagle, "and what shall we have to remember thee by? Leave with us thy silver fork."

He left with them the silver fork and rode away. A first day he rode, a second day he rode, and on the third day, at sun-up, he found himself approaching a third Palace of porphyry, roofed with golden tiles, larger and more elegant than the Hawk's and the Eagle's put together. In front of the Palace stood a birch tree on which sat a Crow. The Crow flew down, alighted on the ground and was transformed into a graceful youth. "Come quickly, Tsarevna Helena," he cried, "our dear brother is coming!" Then Tsarevna Helena came running from the Palace and met her brother joyfully, embracing him with many questions.

With them also the Tsarevich abode three days, when he bade them farewell to continue his search for his wife.

"Thy search may be in vain," said the Crow, "for the Wizard Koschei is very powerful and cunning. We would have something to recall thee to us. Leave with us thy silver snuff-box, so that we may look on it often and know of thy welfare."

Tsarevich Alexis left behind the silver snuffbox and again set out. Whether he rode a long way or a short way, by wet roads or dry, he came at last to the Castle of Koschei, where, walking in the garden, he found his dear one, Maria Morevna. When she saw him, the beautiful Tsar's daughter threw herself on his breast, weeping a flood of tears. "O Tsarevich Alexis!" she cried, "why didst thou disobey my command? Why didst thou open the closet and loose the Wizard to our hurt?"

"I am guilty before thee," answered the Tsarevich sadly. "But remember not the old things which are past. Come with me and let us fly, while Koschei is not to be seen. Perchance he will not be able to overtake us." So without more ado he took her up before him on the saddle and put his good steed to its best pace.

Now that day the Wizard had gone hunting. Toward evening he rode back to his Castle, when suddenly his horse stumbled under him. Thereat he rated it, crying: "Why stumblest thou, sorry nag? Hast thou not been well fed, or dost thou feel some misfortune?"

The horse replied: "Master, I feel a misfortune. Tsarevich Alexis has been here and has carried away thy Maria Morevna."

"Canst thou overtake them?" demanded the Wizard.

"Thou mayest sow a measure of wheat," answered the horse, "thou mayest wait till it is grown, harvest and thresh it, grind the grain to flour, and of it bake five ovens of bread to eat, and even after that I should be able to overtake them."

Koschei put his horse to a gallop and easily overtook Tsarevich Alexis. "Well," he said, "when thou gavest me to drink, I promised on occasion to give thee thy life. Therefore this time I do not slay thee." Then taking Maria Morevna from him, he returned to his Castle, leaving the Tsarevich weeping.

Tsarevich Alexis wept a long time, but weeping was of no avail, and at length he dried his tears and at daybreak on the morrow rode again to the Wizard's Castle.

Koschei was once more gone hunting, and the Tsarevich, finding Maria Morevna in the garden, said: "Come, mount with me and let us fly."

"Gladly would I," she answered, "but the Wizard will overtake us, and I fear he will slay thee."

"At least we shall have had some hours together," said Tsarevich Alexis and, taking her up before him, put spurs to his steed.

In the evening Koschei returned from the hunt, and as he neared his Castle, his horse staggered. "What dost thou, starveling hack!" he said. "Art thou underfed, or dost thou scent some evil?"

"I scent an evil, master," the horse answered. "Tsarevich Alexis has been here and has borne away thy Maria Morevna."

"Canst thou overtake them?" asked the Wizard.

The horse replied: "Thou mayest scatter a measure of barley, wait till it is high, cut it, thresh it, and of the grain brew beer. Thou mayest drink the beer till thou art tipsy and sleep till thou art sober, and still I should be able to overtake them."

The Wizard put his horse to a gallop and before long overtook Tsarevich Alexis. "Did I not tell thee," he said, "that thou shouldst as easily see thine own ears as again to possess Maria Morevna? When thou gavest me water, I promised to give thee twice thy life. Therefore, for the second time, I forbear to slay thee. But for the third time, beware!" So saying he took Maria Morevna and rode back to his Castle, leaving the Tsarevich weeping bitter tears.

Tsarevich Alexis wept till his weeping was ended, and when the next day dawned, for the third time he rode to Koschei's Castle.

This day also the Wizard was absent. He found Maria Morevna and begged her to mount and fly with him. "Most gladly would I," she said, "but the Wizard will overtake us, and this third time he will not spare thee." But he answered: "If I cannot live with thee, I will not live without thee!" So he prevailed on her and took her up before him and spurred away.

When evening had come, Koschei rode home from his hunting, and as he neared his Castle, his horse began to sway from side to side. "How now, thou beggarly cob!" he cried. "Dost thou lack fodder, or dost thou perceive some calamity?"

"I perceive a calamity, master," replied the horse. "Tsarevich Alexis has been here and has ridden away with thy Maria Morevna."

"Canst thou overtake them?" asked the Wizard.

And the horse answered: "Thou mayest strew a measure of flax seed, wait till it is ripe, and pick, clean and card it. Thou mayest spin thread, weave cloth, sew a garment, and wear the garment into shreds, and even then I should be able to overtake them."

Koschei made him gallop and at length overtook the Tsarevich. "Twice I gave thee thy life," he said, "but this third time thou shalt die." He killed his horse with a blow of the sword, dragged the Tsarevich to the Castle, put him in a cask barred and hooped with iron, and threw the cask into the sea-ocean, while Maria Morevna again he took to himself.

Now the Hawk, the Eagle and the Crow used often to look at the silver spoon, the fork and the snuff-box, and wonder how their brother-in-law fared in his search. One day, looking, they saw that the three pieces of silver were turning black, and they said to themselves: "Our dear brother-in-law is in peril of his life."

The Hawk flew at once to the Eagle, and together they sought the Crow. Having made their plan, the Crow flew to the west, the Eagle to the east, and the Hawk to the north, and after searching all day they met together to confer.

"I saw naught to remark," said the Hawk, "save a band of crows flying south."

"I saw and questioned them," said the Crow, "and they replied that they sighted something afloat on the sea-ocean."

"And I saw," said the Eagle, "what it was. It was a cask, barred and bound with hoops of iron."

"Brothers," said the Hawk, "let us see what the cask holds."

They flew together to where the cask floated, pulled it to shore, and with sharp beaks and claws picked and tore it apart, and in it to their delight they found their brother-in-law, the Tsarevich, safe and well. He told them all that had befallen him and begged their counsel.

When they had consulted together, the Crow said: "Our counsel is this. Koschei's horse is a hundredfold swifter than any other, and for this reason, try as oft as thou wilt, he is sure to overtake thee. Find out where it was foaled, and perchance thou mayest obtain another as swift."

Tsarevich Alexis, having thanked them, set out again afoot for the Castle of the Wizard, where Maria Morevna wept tears of joy that he was still alive, and to her he said: "Find out, if thou canst, where Koschei obtained his good horse, and tell me tomorrow."

So that night the beautiful Tsar's daughter said to Koschei: "All things are open to thee, wise Wizard! Tell me, I pray, where was foaled thy marvellous steed which thrice overtook Tsarevich Alexis to his death?"

Koschei said: "On the shore of the blue sea-ocean there is a meadow, and upon it there courses up and down a wonderful mare. Twelve hay-cutters reap the grass of the meadow, and as many more with rakes turn it. The mare follows them, devouring the grass they cut. When she bathes, the sea rises in huge waves, and when she rubs her sides against the oak trees, they fall to the ground like sheaves of oats. Every month she brings forth a foal, and twelve fierce wolves follow her to devour them. Every three years the mare bears a she-colt with a white star on its forehead, and he who, at the moment it is born, snatches away this foal, fights off the wolves from it and brings it safely away, will possess a steed like to mine."

"Didst thou, O Koschei," asked Maria Morevna, "gain thy horse by these means?"

"Not I," the Wizard answered. "Across three times nine lands, in the thirtieth Tsardom, on the further side of the River of Fire, there lives an old Baba Yaga. She follows the mare and snatches away each she-colt which bears on its forehead the white star. She thus has many wonderful horses. I once spent three days tending them, and for reward she gave me a little foal, which became the good horse I ride."

"But how didst thou cross the River of Fire?" asked Maria Morevna.

"As to that," replied the Wizard, "I have in my chest a fine handkerchief. I have only to wave it three times to my right side to have a strong bridge so high that the fire cannot reach it."

Maria Morevna listened attentively, and when Koschei was asleep, she took the fine handkerchief from the chest, brought it to Tsarevich Alexis, and told him all the Wizard had said.

The Tsarevich hastened away, crossed three times nine countries, and in the thirtieth Tsardom came to the River of Fire. By means of the magic handkerchief he crossed it and went on to find the old Baba Yaga.

He walked one day, he walked two days, he walked three days, without either food or drink. When he was like to die from hunger, he came upon a bird with her fledglings. One of these he caught, when the mother bird, flying near, said: "Tsarevich, do not, I pray thee, eat my little one. If thou wilt set it free, one day I will serve thee a service."

The Tsarevich let the fledgling go, and soon thereafter, in a forest, he found a wild bee's hive. He was about to eat the honey when the Queen Bee said: "Tsarevich, do not take the honey, since it is food for my subjects. Leave it to me, and one day, in return, I will serve thee a service."

The Tsarevich left the honey and went on till he came to the sea-ocean, and on the sand he caught a crayfish. When he was about to eat it, however, the crayfish begged for its life. "Do not eat me, Tsarevich," it said, "and one day I will serve thee a service." So he let the crayfish go also and went on his way, so tired and hungry that he could scarcely crawl.

Whether he went a long way or a short way, he came at length, at daybreak, in a forest, to the hut of the old Baba Yaga, turning round and round on hens' legs. About the hut were planted twelve poles. On the tops of eleven were men's heads, but the twelfth had none.

Tsarevich Alexis drew near and said:

> "Little Hut, little Hut!
> "Stand the way thy mother placed thee,
> "With thy back to the wood and thy face to me!"

And when the hut stood still facing him, he climbed up one of the hens' legs and entered. There lay the old witch on the stove, snoring.

The Tsarevich woke her. "Health to thee, grandmother!" he said.

"Health to thee, Tsarevich!" she answered. "Why hast thou come to me? Is it by thine own will or by need?"

"By both," said Tsarevich Alexis. "I come to serve thee as herder, to graze thy she-horses and to earn a colt for my payment."

"Why shouldst thou not?" the Baba Yaga said. "With me folk serve no round year but only three days. If thou dost graze well my mares, I will give thee a steed fit for a hero. But if thou dost lose one of them, thy head shall be set upon my twelfth pole."

Tsarevich Alexis agreed. The old witch gave him food and drink, and ordered him to take her mares to the open field. He opened the stockade, but the instant the mares were free, they whisked their tails and galloped off in different directions, so that they disappeared before he had scarce time to lift his eyes.

Then the Tsarevich began to weep and to lament. He sat down on a stone and after weeping for a long time fell asleep.

When the sun was setting, a bird woke him by pecking at his sleeve. "Rise, Tsarevich Alexis," said the bird; "the mares are all in the stockade. I have served thee the service I promised when thou didst loose my little fledgling."

He thanked the bird and went back to the witch's hut, where the Baba Yaga was shouting at her she-horses. "Why did ye come home?" she cried to them angrily.

"Why should we not?" they answered. "We did thy bidding. We galloped far and further, but flocks of birds came flying from the whole world and came near to pecking out our eyes!"

"Well," she bade them, "tomorrow run not on the meadow but scatter throughout the thick wood."

Tsarevich Alexis slept soundly. In the morning the old witch sent him out again, saying: "Mind thou losest none today, or thy head shall be put upon my pole!"

He opened the stockade, but the moment they were out, the mares switched their tails and set off running into the pathless woods. And again the Tsarevich sat down on a stone and wept until he went to sleep. Scarce, however, had the sun begun to set behind the trees than a great bee came buzzing, woke him and said: "Hasten, Tsarevich Alexis; the mares are all in the stockade, and I have repaid thee for leaving my honey."

He thanked the bee and returned to the hut, where he found the Baba Yaga again scolding her she-horses for returning.

"How could we help it?" they replied. "We obeyed thy command and ran deep into the trackless forest, but thousands of angry bees came flying from the whole world and stung us till our blood came, and pursued us even here."

"Well," she told them, "tomorrow go neither to the meadow nor to the forest, but swim far out into the sea-ocean."

Again Tsarevich Alexis slept soundly, and the next morning came the witch and sent him a third time to graze her mares, saying: "Beware I miss no one of them at night, else shall thy head certainly be set upon my house pole."

He loosed the mares from the stockade, but scarce were they outside when they flirted their tails, and galloping to the blue sea-ocean plunged into the water up to their necks and swam until they were lost to view. And the Tsarevich for a third time sat down on a stone to weep and so fell asleep.

When the sun was low, he woke to find a crayfish nipping his finger. "Come, Tsarevich Alexis," it said, "the she-horses are all safe in their stalls, and I have served thee my service in payment for my life. Return now to the hut but show not thyself to the old witch. Go, rather, into the stable and hide thyself behind the manger. In a corner there thou wilt find a shabby little colt, which is so poor that it drags its hind legs in the mire. When midnight comes, take this little colt and depart to thine own land."

The Tsarevich thanked the crayfish, went back to the hut and hid himself behind the manger. And soon he heard the Baba Yaga rating her she-horses for returning.

"How could we remain in the water?" they answered. "We swam to the very middle of the abyss, but hosts of crayfish came creeping from the whole sea-ocean, and with their claws pinched the flesh from our bones, so that to escape them we gladly would have run to the end of the white world."

The old witch waited and waited for the Tsarevich's return, but at length she fell asleep. At midnight he saddled the shabby colt, led it from the stable and made his way to the River of Fire. He waved the Wizard's handkerchief three times to his right side, and a strong high bridge sprang from bank to bank. He led his colt across it and waved the handkerchief twice to his left side, and the bridge shrank and became thin and narrow, till it was but one-third as high and one-third as strong.

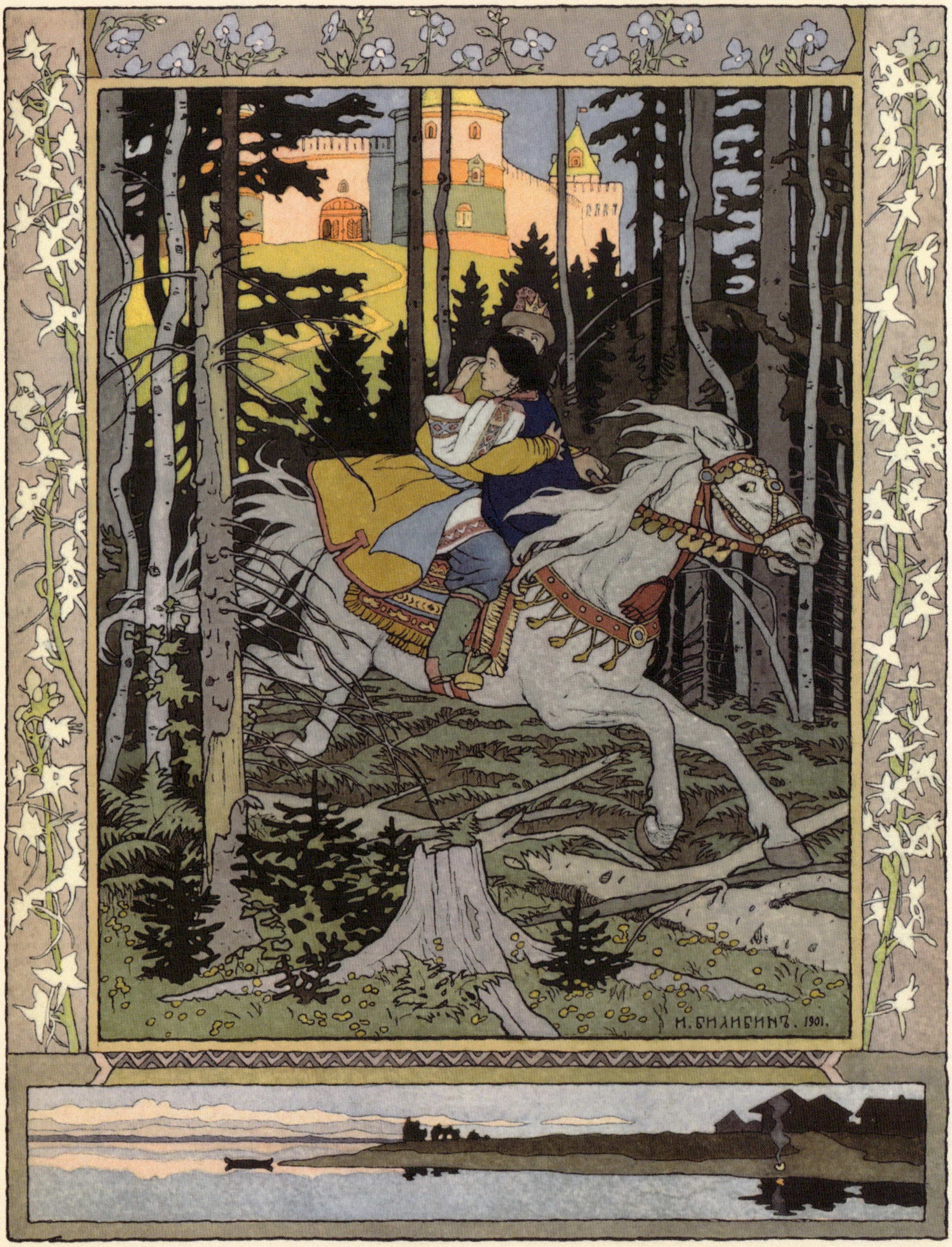
И. БИЛИБИНЪ. 1901.

Now at daybreak the Baba Yaga woke and missed the colt from the stable. She at once sprang into her iron mortar and started in pursuit, driving with her iron pestle and sweeping away the trail behind her with her kitchen broom. She came to the River of Fire and, seeing the bridge, started to cross it. But she had scarce come to the middle when it gave way, and the old witch, falling into the flaming stream beneath, met her instant death.

As for Tsarevich Alexis, he grazed his colt twelve mornings at sunrise on the green meadow, and it became a horse fit for a hero to ride. Then, mounting, he galloped back to the Tsardom of Koschei, to the Wizard's Castle. He found Maria Morevna and said: "Haste and mount before me, for now I have a horse as good as Koschei's!" He took her on the saddle and rode off at full speed.

In the evening when the Wizard returned, as he neared his Castle, his horse fell upon one knee. "What! thou dawdling bag of bones!" he said. "Dost thou stumble again? Art thou weak from emptiness or dost thou smell some mishap?"

"I smell a mishap, master," replied the horse. "Tsarevich Alexis has been here and has ridden away with thy Maria Morevna."

"Canst thou overtake them?" asked Koschei.

"I cannot tell," the horse answered. "The Tsarevich has now for his steed my youngest brother."

The Wizard put his horse at its best pace and galloped in pursuit. Whether he rode a long way or a short way, by rough roads or smooth, at length he overtook them and lifted his sword to cut Tsarevich Alexis in pieces.

At that moment the horse the Tsarevich rode cried to the other: "O my brother! Why dost thou continue to serve such an unclean monster? Cast him from thy back and strike him with thy sharp hoofs." And the horse of Koschei heard the counsel of his brother and threw his rider on the ground and lashed out with his hoofs so cruelly that the Wizard was forced to crawl back to his Castle on all fours.

Then Tsarevich Alexis mounted Koschei's horse, and setting Maria Morevna on his own, they rode to visit his brothers-in-law, the Hawk, the Eagle and the Crow.

At each of the three Palaces they were received with rejoicing. "So thou hast gained thy Maria Morevna," they said. "Well, thou didst not take so much trouble for naught, since were one to search the whole world, he could find no other such a beauty!" And when their visits and feastings were ended, they rode back to the Tsarevich's own Tsardom and lived happily together always and got all good things.

The Feather of Finist the Falcon

Once, in olden times, there was a merchant whose wife had died, leaving him three daughters. The eldest two were plain of face and hard of heart and cared for nothing but finery, while the youngest was a good housekeeper, kind-hearted, and so beautiful that it could neither be told in a tale nor written down with a pen.

One day, when the merchant set out for the Fair, he called his three daughters and asked: "My dear daughters, what do ye most desire me to buy for you?" The eldest answered: "Bring me a piece of rich brocade for a gown." The second said: "Bring me a fine scarf for a shawl." But the youngest replied: "Little father, bring me only a scarlet flower to set in my window."

The two sisters laughed at her request. "Little fool," they said, "what dost thou want of a scarlet flower? Thou wouldst better ask for a new apron." But she paid no heed, and when the merchant asked her again, she said: "Little father, buy for me only the scarlet blossom."

The merchant bade them good-bye and drove to the Fair, and whether in a short while or a long while, he came again to his house. He brought the rich brocade for the eldest daughter and the fine scarf for the second, but he quite forgot to bring the

38

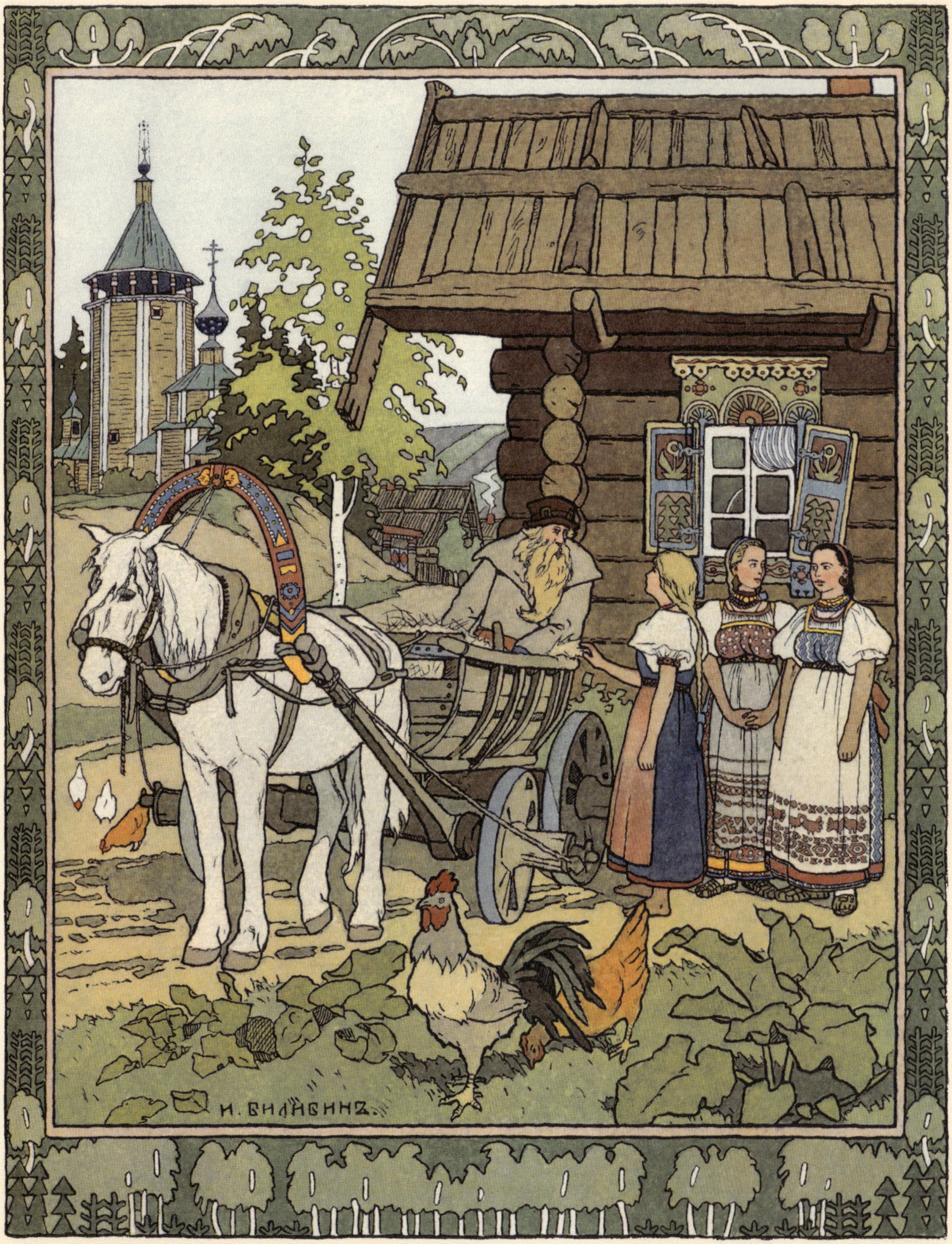
И. БИЛИБИНЪ.

little scarlet flower. The eldest daughters were so rejoiced at their gifts that he felt sorry for his forgetfulness, and said to the youngest to comfort her: "Never mind, I shall soon go again to the Fair and shall bring thee a gift also." And she answered: "It is no matter, little father; another time thou wilt remember." And while her sisters, cutting and sewing their fine stuffs, laughed at her, she was silent.

Time passed, and again the merchant made ready to go to the Fair, and calling his daughters, he asked: "Well, my daughters, what shall I buy for you?" The eldest answered, "Bring me a gold chain," and the second, "Buy me a pair of golden earrings," but the third said, "Little father, I want nothing but a scarlet flower to set in my window."

The merchant went to the Fair and bought for the eldest daughter the chain and for the second the earrings, but again he forgot the scarlet flower. When he returned and the eldest two daughters took joy in their golden jewellery, he comforted the youngest as before, saying: "A simple flower is no great thing. Never mind. When I go again, I shall bring thee a gift." And again she answered: "It is no matter, little father; another time perhaps I shall be luckier."

A third time the merchant made ready to go to the Fair, and called his three daughters and asked them what they most desired. The first answered, "Bring me a pair of satin shoes," the second said, "Buy me a silken petticoat," but the youngest said as before, "Little father, all my desire is for the scarlet flower to set in my window."

The merchant set out to the Fair, and he purchased the pair of satin shoes and the silken petticoat, and then he bethought himself of the scarlet flower and went all about inquiring for one. But search as he might, he could find not a single blossom of that colour in the whole town, and drove home sorrowful that he must disappoint his youngest daughter for the third time.

And as he rode along, wondering where he might find the flower, he met by the roadside in the forest a little old man whom he had never seen, with a hooked nose, one eye, and a face covered with a golden beard like moss, who carried a box on his back.

"What dost thou carry, old man?" he asked.

"In my box," answered the old man, "is a little scarlet flower which I am keeping for a present to the maiden who is to marry my son, Finist the Falcon."

"I do not know thy son, old man," said the merchant, "nor yet the maiden whom he is to marry. But a scarlet blossom is no great thing. Come, sell it to me, and with the money thou mayest buy a more suitable gift for the bridal."

"Nay," replied the little old man. "It has no price, for wherever it goeth there goeth the love of my son, and I have sworn it shall be his wife's."

The merchant argued and persuaded, for now that he had found the flower he was loath to go home without it, and ended by offering in exchange for it both the satin shoes and the silken petticoat, till at length the little old man said: "Thou canst have the scarlet flower for thy daughter only on condition that she weds my son, Finist the Falcon."

The merchant thought a moment. Not to bring the flower would grieve his daughter, yet as the price of it he must promise to wed her to a stranger.

"Well, old man," he said, "give me the flower, and if my daughter will take thy son, he shall have her."

"Have no fear," said the little old man. "Whom my son woos, her will he wed!" and giving the box to the other, he instantly vanished.

The merchant, greatly disturbed at his sudden disappearance, hurried home, where his three daughters came out to greet him. He gave to the eldest the satin shoes and to the second the silken petticoat, and seeing them they clapped their hands for delight. Then he gave to his youngest daughter the little box and said: "Here is thy scarlet flower, my daughter, but as for me, I take no joy of it, for I had it of a stranger, though it was not for sale, and in return for it I have promised that thou shalt wed his son, Finist the Falcon."

"Sorrow not, little father," said she. "Thou hast done my desire, and if Finist the Falcon will woo me, then will I wed him." And she took out the scarlet flower and caressed it, and held it close to her heart.

When night came, the merchant kissed his daughters, made over them the sign of the cross and sent them each to her bed. The youngest locked herself in her room in the attic, took the little flower from its box and, setting it on the window-sill, began to smell it and kiss it and look into the dark blue sky, when suddenly in through the window came flying a swift beautiful falcon with coloured feathers. It lit upon the floor and immediately was transformed into a young Prince, so handsome that it could not be told in speech nor written in a tale.

The Prince soothed her fright and caressed her with sweet and tender words, so that she began to love him with such a joyful heart that one knows not how to tell it. They talked—who can tell of what?—and the whole night passed as swiftly as an hour in the daytime. When the day began to break, Finist the Falcon said to her: "Each evening when thou dost set the scarlet flower in the window, I will come flying to thee. Tonight, ere I fly away as a falcon, take one feather from my wing. If thou hast need of anything, go to the steps under the porch and wave the feather on thy right side, and whatsoever things thy soul desireth, they shall be thine. And when thou hast no longer need of them, wave the feather on thy left side." Then he kissed her and bade her farewell, and turned into a falcon with coloured feathers. She plucked a single bright feather from his wing, and the bird flew out of the window and was gone.

The next day was Sunday, and the elder sisters began to dress in their finery to go to church. "What wilt thou wear, little fool?" they said to the other. "But for thy scarlet flower thou mightst have had a new gown, instead of disgracing us by thy appearance."

"Never mind," she said; "I can pray also here at home." And after they were gone, she sat down at her attic window watching the finely dressed people going to Mass. When the street was empty, she went to the steps under the porch and waved the bright feather to the right side, and instantly there appeared a crystal carriage with high-bred horses harnessed to it, coachmen and footmen in gold livery, and a gown embroidered in all kinds of precious stones. She dressed herself in a moment, sat down in the carriage, and away it went, swift as the wind, to the church.

When she entered, so beautiful she was that all the people turned to look at her. "Some high-born Princess has come!" they whispered to each other; and in her splendid gown and headdress, even her two sisters did not recognize her as the one they had left in her little attic room. As soon as the choir began to sing the Magnificat, she left the church, entered the crystal carriage and drove off so swiftly that when the people flocked out to stare, there was no trace of her to be seen. As soon as she reached home, she took off the splendid gown and put on her own, went to the porch, waved the bright feather to the left side, and the carriage and horses, the coachmen in livery and the splendid gown disappeared, and she sat down again at her attic window.

When the elder sisters returned, they said: "What a beauty came today to church! No one could gaze enough at her. Thou, little slattern, shouldst have seen her rich gown! Surely she must have been a Princess from some other Province!"

Now so hastily had she changed her clothes that she had forgotten to take out of her hair a diamond pin, and her sisters caught sight of it. "What a lovely jewel!" they cried enviously. "Where didst thou get it?" And they would have taken it from her. But she ran to her attic room and hid it in the heart of the scarlet flower, so that though they searched everywhere they could not find it. Then, filled with envy, they went to their father and said: "Sir, our sister hath a secret lover who has given her a diamond ornament, and we doubt not that she will bring shame upon us." But he would not hear them and bade them look to themselves.

That evening when all went to bed, the girl set the flower on the window-sill, and in a moment Finist the Falcon came flying in and was transformed into the handsome Prince, and they caressed one another and talked together till the dawn began to break.

Now the elder sisters were filled with malice and spite, and they listened at the attic door hoping to find where she had hidden the diamond pin, and so heard the voices. They knocked at the door, crying: "With whom dost thou converse, little sister?"

"It is I talking to myself," she answered.

"If that is true, unlock thy door," they said.

Then Finist the Falcon kissed her and bade her farewell, and turning into a falcon, flew out of the window, and she unlocked the door.

Her sisters entered and looked all about the room, but there was no one to be seen. They went, however, to their father and said: "Sir, our sister hath a shameless lover who comes at night into her room. Only just now we listened and heard them conversing." He paid no heed, however, but chided them and bade them better their own manners.

Each night thereafter the spiteful pair stole from their beds to creep to the attic and listen at the door, and each time they heard the sound of the loving talk between their sister and Finist the Falcon. Yet each morning they saw that no stranger was in the room, and at length, certain that whoever entered must do so by the window, they made a cunning plan. One evening they prepared a sweet drink of wine and in it they put a sleeping powder and prevailed on their sister to drink it. As soon as she did so, she fell into a deep sleep; and they laid her on her bed, fastened open knives and sharp needles upright on her window-sill and bolted the window.

When the dark fell, Finist the Falcon came flying to his love, and the needles pierced his breast and the knives cut his brilliant wings, and although he struggled and beat against it, the window remained closed. "My beautiful dearest," he cried, "hast thou ceased so soon to love me? Never shalt thou see me again unless thou searchest through three times nine countries, to the thirtieth Tsardom, and thou shalt first wear through three pairs of iron shoes, and break in pieces three iron staves, and gnaw away three holy church-loaves of stone. Only then shalt thou find thy lover, Finist the Falcon!" But though through her sleep she heard these bitter words, still she could not awaken, and at last the wounded Falcon, hearing no reply, shot up angrily into the dark sky and flew away.

In the morning when she awoke, she saw how the window had been barred with knives set crosswise, and with needles, and how great drops of crimson blood were falling from them, and she began to wring her hands and to weep bitter tears. "Surely," she thought, "my cruel sisters have made my dear love perish!" When she had wept a long time, she thought of the bright feather, and ran to the porch and waved it to the right, crying: "Come to me, my own Finist the Falcon!" But he did not appear, and she knew that the charm was broken.

Then she remembered the words she had heard through her sleep, and telling no one, she went to a smithy and bade the smith make her three pairs of iron shoes and three iron staves, and with these and three church-loaves of stone she set out across three times nine countries to the thirtieth Tsardom.

She walked and walked, whether for a short time or a long time, the telling is easy, but the journey is not soon done. She wandered for a day and a night, for a week, for two months and for three. She wore through one pair of the iron shoes, and broke to pieces one of the iron staves, and gnawed away one of the stone church-loaves, when, in the midst of a wood which grew always thicker and darker, she came to a lawn. On the lawn was a little hut that stood on hens' legs. In the hut lived a sour-faced old woman.

"Whither dost thou hold thy way, beautiful maiden?" asked the old woman.

"O grandmother," answered the girl, "I beg for thy kindness! Be my hostess and cover me from the dark night. I am searching for Finist the bright Falcon, who was my friend."

"Well," said the dame, "he is a relative of mine; but thou wilt have to cross many lands still to find him. Come in and rest for the night. The morning is wiser than the evening."

The old woman gave the girl to eat and drink, a portion of all God had given her, and a bed to sleep on, and in the morning when the dawn began to break, she awoke her. "Finist, who flies as the falcon with coloured feathers," she said, "is now in the fiftieth Tsardom of the eightieth land from here. He has recently proposed marriage to a Tsar's daughter. Thou mayest, perhaps, reach there in time for the wedding feast. Take thou this silver spindle; when thou usest it, it will spin thee a thread of pure gold. Thou mayest give it to his wife for a wedding gift. Go now with God across three times nine lands to the house of my second cousin. I am bad-tempered, but she is worse than I. However, speak with her fair, and she may direct thee further."

The girl thanked the old woman and, bidding her farewell, set out again, though with a heavier heart, on her journey. She walked and walked, whether for a short time or a long time, across green steppe and barren wilderness, until at length, when the second pair of iron shoes were worn through, the second staff broken to pieces and the second stone church-loaf gnawed away, she came one evening, on the edge of a swamp, to a little hut on whose doorstep sat a second old woman, sourer than the first.

"Whither goest thou, lovely girl?" asked the dame.

"O grandmother," she answered, "grant me thy kindness. Be my hostess and protect me from the dark night. I seek my dear friend, who is called Finist the Falcon, whom my cruel sisters wounded and drove from me."

"He is a relative of mine," said the old woman, "but thou wilt have to walk many versts further to find him. He is to marry a Tsar's daughter, and today is her last maiden feast. But enter and rest. The morning is wiser than the evening."

The old woman put food and drink before her and gave her a place to sleep. Early on the morrow she woke her. "Finist the Falcon," she said, "lives in the fiftieth land from here. Take with thee this golden hammer and these ten little diamond nails. When thou usest them, the hammer will drive the nails of itself. If thou choosest, thou mayest give them to his wife for a wedding-gift. Go now with God to the house of my fourth cousin. I am crabbed, but she is more ill-tempered than I. However, greet her with politeness and perhaps she will direct thee further. She lives across three times nine lands, beside a deep river."

The girl took the golden hammer and the ten little diamond nails, thanked the old woman and went on her way. She walked a long way and she walked a short way, and at last, when the third pair of iron shoes were worn through, and the third iron staff broken to pieces, and the third stone church-loaf gnawed away, she came, in a dark wood where the tops of the trees touched the sky, to a deep river and on its bank stood a little hut, on whose doorstep sat a third old woman, uglier and sourer than the other two put together.

"Whither art thou bound, beautiful girl?" asked the dame.

"O grandmother," she answered, "grant me a kindness. Be my hostess and shield me from the dark night! I go to find Finist the Falcon, my dearest friend, whom my sisters pierced with cruel needles and knife blades, and drove away bleeding."

"He is a relative of mine," said the old woman, "and his home is not very far from here. But come in and rest this night; the morning is wiser than the evening."

So the girl entered and ate and drank what the old woman gave her, and slept till daybreak, when the other woke her and said: "Finist the Falcon with coloured feathers is now in the next Tsardom from here, beside the blue sea-ocean, where he stays at the Palace, for in three days he is to marry the Tsar's daughter. Go now with God and take with thee this golden saucer and this little diamond ball. Set the ball on the plate, and it will roll of itself. Mayhap thou wilt wish to give them as a wedding gift to his bride."

She thanked the old woman and started again on her way, and in the afternoon she came to the blue sea-ocean spreading wide and free before her, and beside it she saw a Palace with high towers of white stone, whose golden tops were glowing like fire. Near the Palace a serving-wench was washing a piece of cloth in the sea, whose waves it tinged with red. The girl asked her: "What is it thou dost cleanse?"

The servant answered: "It is a shirt of Finist the Falcon, who in three days will wed my mistress, but it is so stained with blood that I can by no means make it clean." The girl thought, "It is a garment my beloved wore after he was so cruelly wounded by the knives in my window!" And taking it from the other's hands, she began to weep over it, so that the tears washed away every stain and the shirt was as white as snow.

The serving-woman took the shirt back to the Tsar's daughter, who asked her how she had so easily cleansed it, and the woman answered that a beautiful maiden, alone on the sea sand, had wept over it till her tears had made it white. "This is, in truth, a remarkable thing," said the Tsar's daughter; "I would see this girl whose tears can wash away such stains." And summoning her maids and nurses and attendants, she went walking along the shore.

Presently she came where the merchant's daughter sat alone on the soft sand gazing sorrowfully out over the blue sea-ocean, and she accosted her and said: "What grief hast thou that thy tears can wash away blood?"

"I grieve," answered the girl, "because I so long to see the beautiful Finist the Falcon."

Then the Tsar's daughter, being very prideful, tossed her head, saying: "Is that all? Go to the Palace kitchen, and I will let thee serve there; perchance as payment thou mayest catch a glimpse of him as he dines."

So the merchant's daughter entered the Palace and was given a humble place among the servants, and when Finist the Falcon sat down to dine, she put the food before him with her own hands. But he, moody and longing for his lost love, sat without raising his eyes and never so much as saw her or guessed her presence.

After dinner, sad and lonely, she went out to the sea beach, sat down on the soft sand, took her little silver spindle and began to draw out a thread. And in the cool of the evening the Tsar's daughter, with her attendants, came walking there and, seeing that the thread that came from the spindle was of pure gold, said to her: "Maiden, wilt thou sell me that plaything?"

"If thou wilt buy it at my price," answered the girl.

"And what is thy price?" asked the Tsar's daughter.

"Let me sit through one night by the side of thy promised husband," said the girl.

Now the Tsar's daughter was cold and deceitful, and desired Finist the Falcon, not because she loved him, but because of his beauty and her own pride. "There can be no harm in that," she thought, "for I will put in his hair an enchanted pin, by reason of which he will not waken, and with the spindle I can cover myself and my mother with gold." So she agreed, and that night, when Finist the Falcon was asleep, she put in his hair the enchanted pin, brought the girl to his room, and said: "Give me now the spindle, and in return thou mayest sit here till daybreak and keep the flies from him."

All night the girl bent over the bed, where the handsome youth lay sleeping, and wept bitter tears. "Awake and rise, Finist, my bright Falcon!" she cried. "I have come at last to thee. I have left my father and my cruel sisters, and I have searched through three times nine lands and a hundred Tsardoms for thee, my beloved!" But Finist slept on and heard nothing, and so the whole long night passed away.

And with the dawn came the Tsar's daughter and sent the girl back to the kitchen, and then took away the enchanted pin so that Finist the Falcon should awaken.

When he came from his chamber, the Tsar's daughter said to him: "Hast thou rested well and art thou refreshed?"

He answered: "I slept, but it seemed to me that someone was beside me all night, weeping and lamenting and beseeching me to awaken, yet I could not arouse myself, and because of that my head is heavy."

And she said: "Thou wert but dreaming! No one has been beside thee!" So Finist the Falcon called for his horse and betook himself to the open steppe a-hunting.

As it happened before, so it befell that day also. Finist the Falcon had no eyes for the girl who waited on him at table, and in the evening, sad and sorrowful, she went out to the blue sea-ocean, and, sitting down on the soft sand, took out the golden hammer and the ten diamond nails and began to play with them. A little later the Tsar's daughter, with her maids and attendants, came walking along the beach, and seeing how the hammer drove the nails by itself, coveted the plaything and desired to buy it.

"It shall be thine," said the girl, "if thou wilt pay me my price."

"And what is the price?" asked the Tsar's daughter.

"Let me watch a second night beside the bed of thy promised husband."

"So be it," said the Tsar's daughter; and that night, after Finist the Falcon had fallen asleep, she put into his hair the enchanted pin, so that he could not waken, and brought the girl to his room. "Give me, now, the golden hammer and the diamond nails," she said, "and thou mayest keep the flies from him till day-dawn."

So that night, too, the merchant's daughter leaned over her beloved through the long dark hours, weeping and crying to him: "Finist my love, my bright Falcon, awake and speak to me! I have come at last to thee! I have journeyed to the fiftieth Tsardom of the eightieth land, and have washed the blood from thy shirt with my

48

tears!" But because of the enchanted pin, Finist could not waken, and at daybreak the girl was sent back to her place in the kitchen.

When Finist came from his chamber, the Tsar's daughter said: "Hast thou slept soundly and art thou refreshed?"

He replied: "I slept, but it seemed to me that the one I loved well bent over me, shedding bitter tears and begging me to arise, yet I could not wake. And because of this my own heart is heavy."

And she said: "It was but a dream that today's hunting will make thee speedily forget. No one was near thee while thou didst sleep." So Finist the Falcon called for his horse and rode to the open steppe.

That day the merchant's daughter wept and was exceeding sorrowful, for on the morrow Finist the Falcon was to be wed. "Never again shall I have the love of my bright falcon!" she thought. "Never more, because of my cruel sisters, may I call him to me with the little scarlet flower in my window!" When evening came, however, she dried her tears, sat down for a third time on the soft sand by the blue sea-ocean and, taking out the golden plate, set the diamond ball upon it. That evening also the Tsar's daughter, with her serving-women, came walking on the beach, and as soon as she saw how the little diamond ball was rolling, rolling of itself, she coveted it and said: "Wilt thou sell these also for the same price as thou didst ask for thy other playthings?"

"Thou shalt have them," answered the merchant's daughter, "for the same price. Let me only sit through this third night by the side of thy promised husband."

"What a fool is this girl!" thought the Tsar's daughter. "Presently I shall have all her possessions and Finist the Falcon for my husband into the bargain!" So she assented gladly, and when Finist the Falcon fell asleep that night, for the third time she put into his hair the enchanted pin and brought the girl into his room, bidding her give over the golden plate and the diamond ball, and keep the flies from him till daybreak.

Through that long night also, the merchant's daughter bent over her loved one, weeping and crying: "Finist, my own dear, my bright Falcon with coloured feathers, awake and know me! I have worn through the three pairs of iron shoes, I have broken to pieces the three iron staves, I have gnawed away the three stone church-loaves, all the while searching for thee, my love!" But by reason of the enchanted pin, although he heard through his sleep her crying and lamenting, and his heart grieved because of it, Finist the Falcon could not waken. So at length, when day-dawn was near, the girl said to herself: "Though he shall never be mine, yet in the past he loved me, and for that I shall kiss him once before I go away," and she put her arms about his head to kiss him. As she did so, her hand touched the pin in his hair and she drew it out, lest by chance it harm him. Thus the spell of its enchantment was broken, and one of her tears, falling on his face, woke him.

And instantly, as he awoke, he recognized her and knew that it was her lamenting he had heard through his sleep. She related to him all that had occurred, how her sisters had plotted, how she had journeyed in search of him, and how she had bought of the Tsar's deceitful daughter the three nights by his side in exchange for the silver spindle, the golden hammer and nails, and the diamond ball that rolled of itself. Hearing, Finist the Falcon was angered against the Tsar's daughter whom he had so nearly wed; but the merchant's daughter he kissed on the mouth and, turning into the falcon, set her on his coloured wings and flew to his own Tsardom.

Then he summoned all his princes and nobles and his officers of all ranks and told them the story, asking: "Which of these two am I to wed? With which can I spend a long life so happily that it will seem a short one: with her who would deceitfully sell my hours for playthings, or with her who sought me over three times nine lands? Do ye now discuss and decide."

And all cried with one voice: "Thou shouldst leave the seller of thy rest and wed her who did follow thee!"

And so did Finist, the bright falcon with coloured wings.

THE FROG PRINCESS

In olden time, in a time long before present days, in a certain Tsardom of an Empire far across the blue seas and behind high mountains, there lived a Tsar and his Tsaritsa. The Tsar had lived long in the white world and through long living had become old. He had three sons, Tsareviches, all of them young, brave and unmarried, and altogether of such a sort that they could not be described by words spoken in a tale or written down with a pen. During the long white days they flew about on their fiery, beautiful horses, like bright hawks under the blue sky. All three were handsome and clever, but the handsomest and cleverest was the youngest, and he was Tsarevich Ivan.

One day the Tsar summoned his three sons to his presence and said: "My dear children, ye have now arrived at man's estate, and it is time for you to think of marriage. I desire you to select maidens to be loving wives to you and to me dutiful daughters-in-law. Take, therefore, your well-arched bows and arrows which have been hardened in the fire. Go into the untrodden field wherein no one is permitted to hunt, draw the bows tight and shoot in different directions, and in whatsoever courts the arrows fall, there demand your wives-to-be. She who brings to each his arrow shall be his bride."

So the Tsareviches made arrows, hardened them in the fire and, going into the untrodden field, shot them in different directions. The eldest brother shot to the east, the second to the west, and the youngest, Tsarevich Ivan, drew his bow with all his strength and shot his arrow straight before him.

On making search, the eldest brother found that his arrow had fallen in the courtyard of a Boyar, where it lay before the tower in which were the apartments of the maidens. The second brother's arrow had fallen in the courtyard of a rich merchant who traded with foreign countries, and it pierced a window at which the merchant's daughter—a lovely girl—was standing. But the arrow of Tsarevich Ivan could not be found at all.

Tsarevich Ivan searched in deep sorrow and grief. For two whole days he wandered in the woods and fields, and on the third day he came by chance to a boggy swamp, where the black soil gave way under the foot, and in the middle of the swamp he came upon a great frog which held in her mouth the arrow he had shot.

When he saw this, he turned to run away, leaving his arrow behind him, but the frog cried: "Kwa! Kwa! Tsarevich Ivan, come to me and take thine arrow. If thou wilt not take me for thy wife, thou wilt never get out of this marsh."

Ivan was greatly surprised to hear the frog speak and was at a loss to know what to do. But at last he took the arrow, picked up the frog, put her in a fold of his coat and went sadly home.

When he arrived at the Palace and told his story, his brothers jeered at him, and the two beautiful maidens whom they were to marry laughed at him also, so that he went weeping to the Tsar and said: "How can I ever take this frog to wife—a little thing that says 'Kwa! Kwa!' She is not my equal. To live one's life long is not like crossing a river or walking over a field. How shall I live with a frog?"

But the Tsar made answer: "Take her, for such was my royal word and such is thy fate!" And though Tsarevich Ivan wept a long time, there was no further word to be said, since one cannot go contrary to his fate.

So the sons of the Tsar were married—the eldest to the nobleman's daughter, the second to the daughter of the merchant, and the youngest, Tsarevich Ivan, was married to the frog. When the day came, he went to the Palace in a closed carriage, and the frog was carried on a golden dish.

So they lived, a long time or a short time, and Tsarevich Ivan treated the frog with gentleness and kindness till a day came when the Tsar summoned his three

И. Билибинъ.

sons before him and said: "Dear children, now that ye are wedded, I am minded to try the skill of my daughters-in-law in the arts of housewifery. Take from my storeroom, therefore, each of you, a piece of linen cloth; each of you shall bid his own wife make a shirt and bring it to me tomorrow morning."

The two elder brothers took the linen to their wives, who at once called together their maidservants and nurses, and all set to work busily to cut the stuff and to sew it. And as they worked, they laughed to think of Tsarevich Ivan, saying: "What will his little frog make for him to bring to the Tsar tomorrow?"

And Tsarevich Ivan went home looking as if he had swallowed a needle. "How can my little frog-wife make a shirt?" he thought—"she who only creeps on the floor and croaks!" And his bright head hung down lower than his shoulders.

When she saw him, however, the frog spoke: "Kwa! Kwa! Tsarevich Ivan, why art thou so downcast? Hast thou heard from the Tsar thy father a hard, unpleasant word?"

"How can I fail to be downcast?" answered Ivan. "The Tsar, my father, has ordered that thou shouldst sew a shirt out of this linen for him tomorrow."

"Worry not," said the frog, "and have no fear. Go to bed and rest. There is more wisdom in the morning than in the evening!"

When Tsarevich Ivan had laid himself down to sleep, she called servants and bade them cut the linen he had brought into small pieces. Then dismissing them, she took the pieces in her mouth, hopped to the window and threw them out, saying: "Winds! Winds! Fly abroad with these linen shreds and sew me a shirt for the Tsar, my father-in-law!" And before one could tell it, back into the room flew a shirt all stitched and finished.

Next morning, when Tsarevich Ivan awoke, the frog presented him with a shirt. "There it is," she said. "Take it to thy father and see if it pleases him." Ivan was greatly rejoiced and, putting the shirt under his coat, set out to the Palace, where his two elder brothers had already arrived.

First of all the eldest brother presented his shirt to his father. The Tsar took it, examined and said: "This is sewn in the common way—it is fit only to be worn in a poor man's hut!" He took the shirt which the second son had brought and said: "This is sewn somewhat better than the other and is perhaps good enough for me to wear when I go to my bath." But when he took the shirt that Tsarevich Ivan presented him, he examined it with delight, for no single seam could be seen in it. He could not admire it enough and gave orders that it should be given him to wear only on the greatest holidays.

Ivan went home happy, but his two brothers said to one another: "We need not laugh at Ivan's wife; she is not really a frog, but a witch."

A second time the Tsar summoned his three sons and said: "My dear children, I wish to taste bread baked by the hands of my daughters-in-law. Bring me tomorrow morning, therefore, each of you a loaf of soft white bread."

Tsarevich Ivan returned home looking very sad, and his bright head hung lower than his shoulders; and when the frog saw him, she said:

"Kwa! Kwa! Kworax! Tsarevich Ivan, why art thou so sad? Hast thou heard a harsh, unfriendly word from the Tsar thy father?"

"Why should I not be sad?" answered Ivan. "The Tsar my father has bidden that thou bake him for tomorrow a loaf of soft white bread."

"Mourn not, Tsarevich Ivan. Be not sad for nothing. Go to bed and sleep in comfort. The morning is wiser than the evening."

When he was asleep, she ordered servants to bring a pastry pot, put flour and cold water into it and make a paste. This she bade them put the pot into the cold oven, and when they were gone, she hopped before the oven door and said:

"Bread, Bread! Be baked!
"Clean, white, and soft as snow!"

Instantly the oven door flew open and the loaf rolled out, cooked crisp and white.

Now the two Tsarevnas, the wives of the other brothers, hated the frog because of the shirt she had made, and when they heard the command of the Tsar, the wife of the eldest brother sent a little slave girl to spy on the frog and see what she would do. The slave girl hid herself where she could watch, and went and told her mistress what she had seen and heard. Then the two Tsarevnas tried to imitate the frog. They dissolved their flour in cold water, poured the paste into cold ovens and repeated over and over again:

"Bread, Bread! Be baked!
"Clean, white, and soft as snow!"

But the ovens remained cold, and the paste would not bake.

Seeing this, in anger they gave the poor slave girl a cruel beating, ordered more flour, made paste with hot water and heated the ovens. But the spilled paste had flowed all about and clogged the flues and made them useless, so that one Tsarevna had her loaf burned on one side and the other took hers out under-baked.

In the morning, when Tsarevich Ivan awoke, the frog sent him to the Palace with his bread wrapped in a towel, and the brothers came also with theirs.

The Tsar cut the loaf of the eldest son and tasted it. "Such bread," he said, "might be eaten only out of misery," and he sent it to the kitchen that it might be given to the beggars. He tasted that of the second son and said: "Give this to my hounds." When Tsarevich Ivan unwrapped his loaf, however, all exclaimed in admiration. For it was so splendid that it would be impossible to make one like it—it could only be told of in tales. It was adorned with all kinds of cunning designs, and on its sides were wrought the Tsar's cities with their high walls and gates. The Tsar tasted it and sent it away, saying: "Put this on my table on Easter Sunday, when we shall have royal visitors." So Ivan went home rejoicing.

A third time the Tsar sent for his three sons and said to them: "My dear children, it is fitting that all women should know how to weave and broider in gold and silver, and I would see if thy wives are skilled also in this. Take, therefore, each of you, from my storehouse silk, gold and silver, and tomorrow morning bring me each of you a carpet."

When Tsarevich Ivan brought sadly home the silk, the gold, and the silver, the frog was sitting on a chair. "Kwa! Kwa! Kworax!" she said. "Tsarevich Ivan, why dost thou mourn? And why doth thy bright head hang down lower than thy shoulders? Hast thou heard from the Tsar thy father a cruel and bitter word?"

"Have I not cause to mourn?" he answered. "The shirt thou hast sewn, and the bread thou has baked; but now my father has bidden that thou make for tomorrow a carpet of this gold, silver, and silk."

"Fret not, Tsarevich Ivan," said the frog. "Lay thee down and rest. The day has more wisdom than the night."

As soon as he was asleep, she called servants and bade them take scissors and cut to pieces all the silk, the gold, and the silver, and then, sending them away, threw it out of the window, and said: "Winds! Winds! fly abroad with these pieces of silk, of gold, and of silver, and make me a carpet such as my dear father used to cover his windows!" And hardly had she said the last word, when back into the room flew an embroidered carpet.

Now again the wives of the elder brothers had sent the little slave girl to watch, and she ran quickly to tell them. And they, thinking that this time the charm must work, cut all of their silk and precious thread into pieces, threw them out of the window, and repeated: "Winds! Winds! fly abroad with these pieces of silk, of gold, and of silver, and make us carpets such as our dear fathers used to cover their windows."

But though they waited a long time, the winds brought them no carpets. Then the Tsarevnas, angry at the loss of their rich threads, after beating the little slave girl more cruelly than before, sent servants hastily for more material, called together their nurses and maidens to help them, and began to work at weaving and embroidering.

In the morning, when Tsarevich Ivan arose, the frog sent him to the Palace to show his carpet with his brothers.

The Tsar looked at the carpet of the eldest son and said: "Take this to the stables. It will do to cover my poorest horse when it is raining." He looked at the carpet of the second and said: "Put this in the hall; it may do, perhaps, to wipe my boots upon in bad weather." But when Tsarevich Ivan unrolled his carpet, so wondrously was it adorned with gold and silver fashionings, that its like cannot be imagined. And the Tsar ordered that it be kept with the greatest care, to be put on his own table on the most solemn feast days.

"Now, my dear children," he said, "your wives, my daughters-in-law, have done all that I bade them do. Bring them tomorrow, therefore, to the Palace to dine, in order that I may congratulate them in person."

The two elder brothers went home to their wives, saying to one another: "Now he must bring his frog-wife with him to the royal audience for all to see!" But Tsarevich Ivan went home weeping, and his bright head hung down lower than his shoulders.

When he reached home, the frog was sitting at the door. "Kwa! Kwa! Kworax!" she said. "Tsarevich Ivan, why dost thou weep? Hast thou heard sharp and unfeeling words from the Tsar thy father?"

"Why should I not weep?" he answered. "Thou hast sewn the shirt, thou hast baked the bread, and thou hast woven the carpet; but after all thou art but a frog, and the Tsar my father commands that I bring thee tomorrow to the Palace to royal audience. How, to my shame, can I show thee to the people as my wife?"

"Weep no more," the frog said. "Go to thy bed and sleep. There is more wisdom in the morning than in the evening."

The next day when Tsarevich Ivan awoke, she said: "Pay no heed to what others think. The Tsar thy father was pleased with his shirt, his bread and his carpet; maybe he will be pleased also with his daughter-in-law when I shall come. Do thou go to the Palace, and I will come after thee in an hour. Make thy respects to the Tsar, and when thou hearest a rumbling and a knocking, say: 'Hither comes my poor little frog in her little basket!'"

So Ivan drove away to the Palace somewhat cheered by her words.

When he was out of sight, the frog went to the window and called: "Winds! Winds! bring for me at once a rich carriage of state, with white horses, footmen, outriders and runners!"

Instantly a horn blew and horsemen came galloping up the street, followed by six milk-white horses drawing a golden coach. As for herself, she threw off the skin of a frog and was transformed into a maiden so beautiful that she could be described neither by words in a tale nor with a pen in writing.

Meanwhile at the Palace the company were assembled, the two elder brothers with their lovely brides attired in silks and laden with shining jewels. And they all laughed at Tsarevich Ivan standing alone, saying: "Where is thy wife, the Tsarevna? Why didst thou not bring her in a kitchen cloth? And art thou certain that thou didst choose the greatest beauty of the swamp?" But while they jeered at poor Ivan, suddenly there came a great rumbling and shouting. The Tsar supposed some King or Prince was arriving to visit him, but Tsarevich Ivan said: "Be not disturbed, father. It is only my poor little frog coming in her little basket."

Nevertheless everybody ran to the Palace windows and saw riders galloping. A golden coach drawn by six milk-white horses flew up to the entrance, and out of it came the lovely maiden—such a beauty as to make the sun and moon ashamed when she looked at them. She came to Tsarevich Ivan, and he took her hand and led her to the Tsar his father, and the Tsar himself seated her at the royal table to dine.

As all began to feast and make merry, the wives of the elder sons whispered among themselves and said: "It is as we have thought. She is in truth a witch. Let us watch carefully, and whatever she does let us be careful to do likewise. So, watching, they saw that the frog-wife did not drink the dregs of her wine cup but poured them in her left sleeve, and that the bones of the roast swan she put in her right sleeve, and they did the same.

When they rose from the table, the musicians began to play and the Tsar led out Ivan's beautiful wife to dance. This she did with exceeding grace. And as she danced, she waved her left sleeve, and at one end of the banquet hall a lake appeared one rod deep. She waved her right sleeve, and swans and geese appeared swimming on it. The Tsar and his guests were astonished and could not sufficiently praise her cleverness. When she finished dancing, the lake and the fowls upon it disappeared.

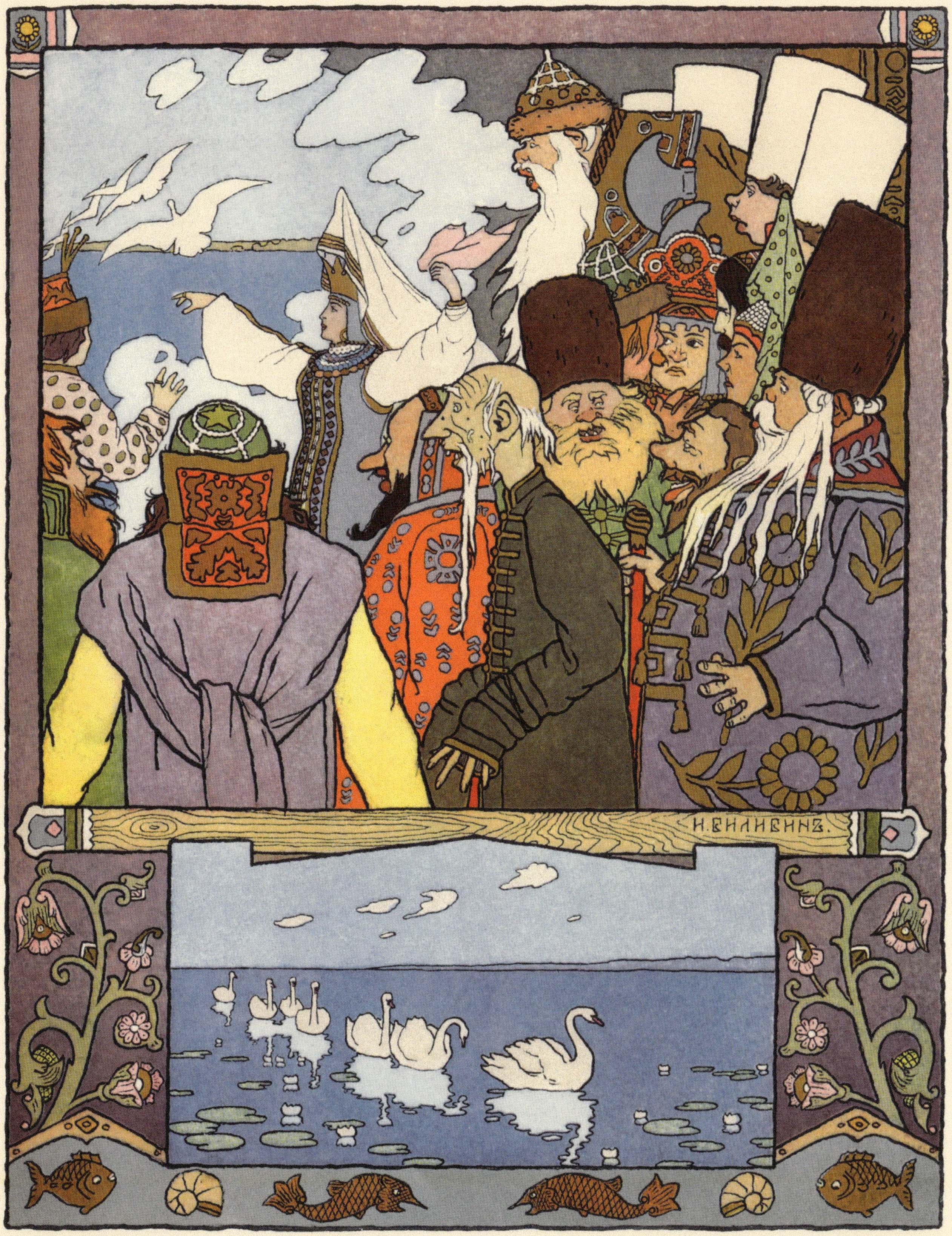
И. БИЛИБИНЪ.

Then the wives of the elder sons began to dance. They waved their left sleeves, and all the guests were splashed with the wine dregs; they waved their right sleeves, and the bones flew right and left, and one nearly put out one of the Tsar's eyes. At this he was angered and straightway ordered them out of the Palace, so that they went home in shame and dishonour.

Now seeing what a beautiful creature his little frog-wife had become, Tsarevich Ivan thought to himself: "What if she should turn back into a frog again!" And while they were dancing, he hastened home, searched till he found the frog-skin and threw it into the fire.

His wife, arriving, ran to search for the skin, and when she could not find it, guessed what he had done.

She immediately fell a-weeping and said: "Alas, alas, Tsarevich Ivan, that thou couldst not have patience even for a little while! Now thou hast lost me forever, unless thou canst find me beyond three times nine lands, in the thirtieth Tsardom, in the empire that lies under the sun. Know that I am the fairy Vasilisa the Wise." When she had said this, she turned into a blue dove and flew out of the window.

Tsarevich Ivan wept till his tears were like a river; then he said a prayer to God and, bidding the Tsar his father and the Tsaritsa his mother farewell, went whither his eyes looked, in search of his lost wife.

He went on and on; whether it was near or far, or a short road or a long road, a tale is soon told, but such a journey is not made quickly. He travelled through thrice nine lands, asking everyone he met where he could find Vasilisa the Wise, but none could answer, till he reached the empire that lies under the sun, and there in the thirtieth Tsardom he met an old grey-beard to whom he told his story and asked his question.

"Well do I know of Vasilisa the Wise," answered the old man. "She is a powerful fairy whose father, in a fit of anger, turned her into a frog for three years. The time was almost up, and hadst thou not burned her frog skin she would be with thee now. I cannot tell thee where she is, but take thou this magic ball, which will roll wherever thou commandest it, and follow it."

Tsarevich Ivan thanked the old grey-beard, threw the ball he gave him on the ground, and at his command it straightway began to roll. It rolled a short way and it rolled a long way, it rolled across a pebbly plain and into a drear and dreadful forest, and in the middle of the forest he came to a little hut that stood on hens' legs and turned continually round and round. Ivan said to it:

> "Little Hut, little Hut!
> "Stand the way thy mother placed thee,
> "With thy back to the wood and thy front to me!"

And immediately the hut turned about facing him and stood still.

Tsarevich Ivan climbed up one of its hens' legs and entered the door, and there he saw the oldest of the Baba Yagas, the grandmother of all the witches, lying on a corner of the stove on nine bricks, with one lip on the shelf, her nose thrust up the chimney, and her huge iron mortar in the corner.

"Poo!" she cried, gnashing her teeth. "Who is this comes to me? Until now I have neither seen with my eyes nor heard with my ears the spirit of any Russian; but to-day it is a Russian who enters my house! Well, Tsarevich Ivan, camest thou hither from thine own wish, or because thou wast compelled?"

"Enough by my own will and twice as much by force," answered Tsarevich Ivan. "But for shame, thou, that thou hast not offered me to eat and to drink, and prepared me a bath!"

Then the Baba Yaga, being pleased with his spirit, gave him food and drink and made ready a bath for him; and when he had refreshed himself, he related to her the whole affair just as it had been. And when she learned that Vasilisa the Wise was

61

in truth his wife, she said: "I will indeed render thee this service, not for love of thee, but because I hate her father. The fairy flies across this forest every day, bringing messages for her father, and stops in my house to rest. Remain here, and as soon as she enters, seize her by the head. When she feels herself caught, she will turn into a frog, and from a frog to a lizard, and from a lizard to a snake, and last of all she will transform herself into an arrow. Do thou take the arrow and break it into three pieces, and she will be thine forever! But take heed when thou hast hold of her not to let her go."

The Baba Yaga concealed the Tsarevich behind the stove, and scarcely was he hidden when in flew Vasilisa the Wise. Ivan crept up noiselessly behind her and seized her by the head. She instantly turned into a great green frog, and he laughed with joy to see her in the form he knew so well. When she turned into a lizard, however, the cold touch of the creature was so loathsome that he let go his hold, and immediately the lizard darted through a crack in the floor.

The Baba Yaga upbraided him. "How shouldst thou win back such a wife," she said, "thou who canst not touch the skin of a creeping lizard? As thou couldst not keep her, thou shalt never again see her here. But if thou likest, go to my sister and see if she will help thee."

Tsarevich Ivan did so. The ball rolled a long way and it rolled a short way, across a mountain and into a deep ravine, and here he came to a second wretched little hovel turning round on hens' legs. He made it stand still and entered it as before, and there on the stove, with one lip on the shelf and her nose propping the ceiling, was the skinny grandaunt of all the witches.

To her he told his story, and for the sake of her sister the Baba Yaga also agreed to help him. "Vasilisa the Wise," she said, "rests in my house too, but if this time thou lettest go thy hold, thou mayest never clasp her more."

So she hid Tsarevich Ivan, and when Vasilisa came flying in, he sprang upon her and seized her and did not flinch even when she turned into a lizard in his hands. But when he beheld the lizard change to a fierce and deadly snake, he cried out in alarm and loosed his hold, and the snake wriggled through the doorway and disappeared.

Then Tsarevich Ivan was exceeding sorrowful, so that he did not even hear the reproaches of the old witch. So bitterly did he weep that she pitied him and said: "Little enough dost thou deserve this wife of thine, but if thou choosest, go to my younger sister and see if she will help thee. For Vasilisa the Wise stops to rest also at her house." So, plucking up heart somewhat, Tsarevich Ivan obeyed.

The ball rolled a long way and it rolled a short way; it crossed a broad river, and there on the shore Tsarevich Ivan came to a third hut, wretcheder than the other two put together, turning round on hens' legs, and in it was the second grandaunt of all the witches. She, too, consented to aid him. "But remember," she said, "if this time thy heart fails and thy hand falters, never again shalt thou behold thy wife in the white world!"

So a third time Tsarevich Ivan hid himself, and presently in came flying Vasilisa the Wise, and this time he said a prayer to God as he sprang out and seized her in a strong grasp. In vain she turned into a frog, into a cold lizard and into a deadly writhing snake. Ivan's grip did not loosen. At last she turned into an arrow, and this he immediately snatched and broke into three pieces. At the same moment, lovely Vasilisa, in her true maiden shape, appeared and threw herself into his arms. "Now, Tsarevich Ivan," she said, "I give myself up to thy will!"

The Baba Yaga gave them for a present a white mare, which could fly like the wind, and on the fourth day it set them down safe and sound at the Tsar's Palace.

He received them with joy and thankfulness, and made a great feast, and after that he made Tsarevich Ivan Tsar in his stead.

Tsarevich Ivan, the Firebird, and the Grey Wolf

In a certain far-away Tsardom not in this Empire, there lived a Tsar named Vyslav, who had three sons: the first Tsarevich Dimitry, the second Tsarevich Vasily, and the third Tsarevich Ivan.

The Tsar had a walled garden, so rich and beautiful that in no kingdom of the world was there a more splendid one. Many rare trees grew in it whose fruits were precious jewels, and the rarest of all was an apple tree whose apples were of pure gold, and this the Tsar loved best of all.

One day he saw that one of the golden apples was missing. He placed guards at all the gates of the garden; but in spite of this, each morning on counting he found one more apple gone. At length he set men on the wall to watch day and night, and these reported to him that every night there came flying into the garden a bird that shone like the moon, whose feathers were gold and its eyes like crystal, which perched on the apple tree, plucked a golden apple and flew away.

Tsar Vyslav was greatly angered and, calling to him his two eldest sons, said: "My dear children, I have for many days sought to decide which of you should inherit

64

my Tsardom and reign after me. Now, therefore, to the one of you who will catch the Firebird, which is the thief of my golden apples, and will bring it to me alive, I will during my life give the half of the Tsardom, and he shall rule after me when I am dead."

The two sons, hearing, rejoiced and shouted with one voice: "Gracious Sir! We shall not fail to bring you the Firebird alive!"

Tsarevich Dimitry and Tsarevich Vasily cast lots to see who should have the first trial, and the lot fell to the eldest, Tsarevich Dimitry, who at evening went into the garden to watch. He sat down under the apple tree and watched till midnight; but when midnight was passed, he fell asleep.

In the morning the Tsar summoned him and said: "Well, my son, didst thou see the Firebird who steals my golden apples?" Being ashamed to confess that he had fallen asleep, however, Tsarevich Dimitry answered: "No, gracious Sir; last night the bird did not visit thy garden."

The Tsar, however, went himself, counted the apples and saw that one more had been stolen.

On the next evening Tsarevich Vasily went into the garden to watch, and he, too, fell asleep at midnight, and next morning when his father summoned him, he, like his brother, being ashamed to tell the truth, answered: "Gracious Sir, I watched throughout the night, but the Firebird that steals the golden apples did not enter thy garden."

And again Tsar Vyslav went himself, counted and saw that another golden apple was missing.

On the third evening Tsarevich Ivan asked permission to watch in the garden, but his father would not permit it. "Thou art but a lad," he said, "and mightest be frightened in the long dark night." But Ivan continued to beseech him till at length the Tsar consented.

So Tsarevich Ivan took his place in the garden and sat down to watch under the apple tree that bore the golden apples. He watched an hour, he watched two hours, he watched three hours. When midnight drew near, sleep almost overcame him, but he drew his dagger and pricked his thigh with its point till the pain aroused him. And suddenly, an hour after midnight, the garden became bright as if lit with the light of many fires, and the Firebird came flying on its golden wings to alight on the lowest bough of the apple tree.

Tsarevich Ivan crept nearer, and as it was about to pluck a golden apple in its beak, he sprang toward it and seized its tail. The bird, however, beating with its golden wings, tore itself loose and flew away, leaving in his hand a single long feather. He wrapped this in a handkerchief, lay down on the ground and went to sleep.

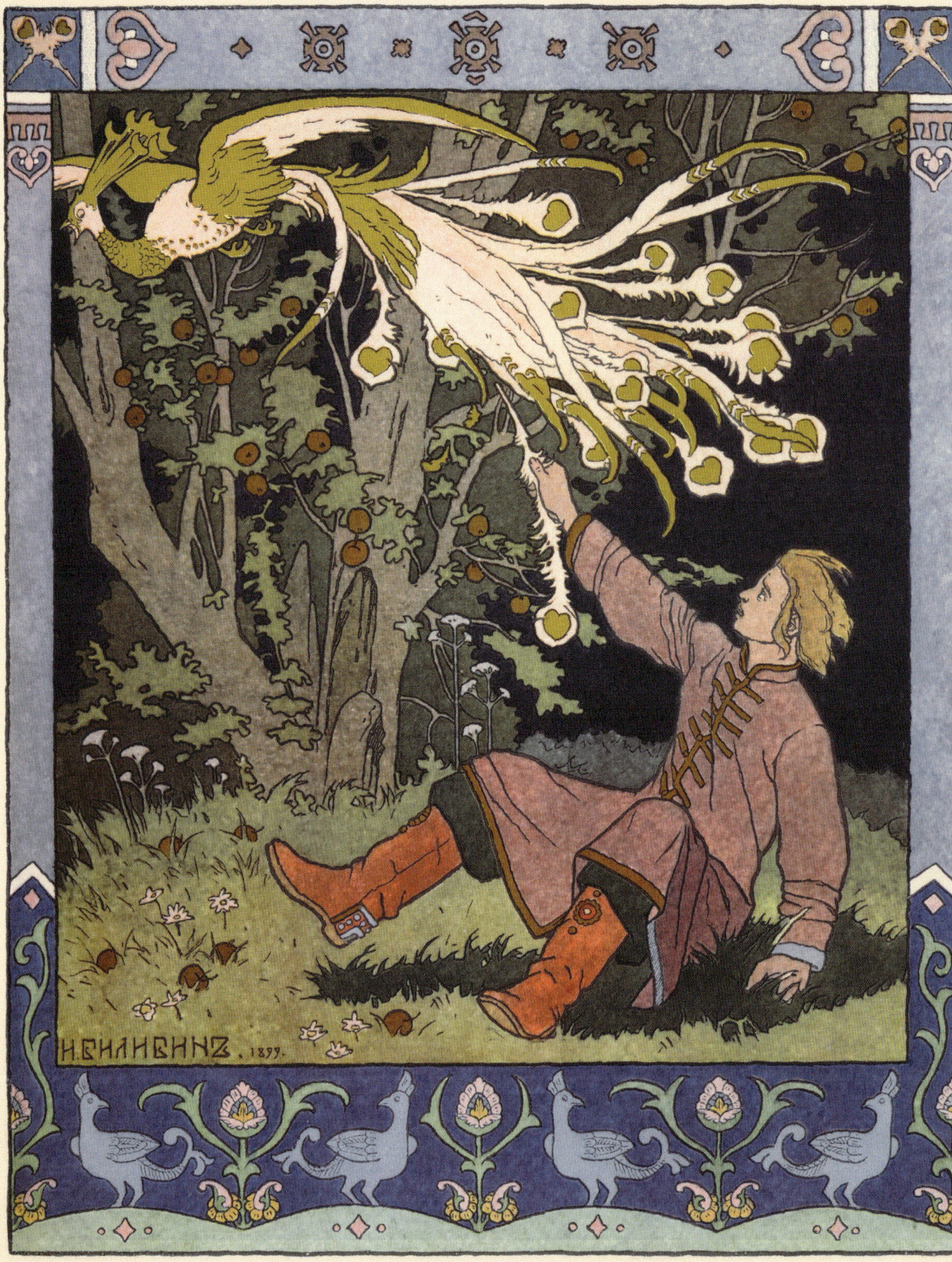
И.БИЛИБИНЪ. 1899.

In the morning Tsar Vyslav summoned him to his presence and said: "Well, my dear son, thou didst not, I suppose, see the Firebird?"

Then Tsarevich Ivan unrolled the handkerchief, and the feather shone so that the whole place was bright with it. The Tsar could not sufficiently admire it, for when it was brought into a darkened room, it gleamed as if a hundred candles had been lighted. He put it into his royal treasury as a thing which must be safely kept forever, and set many watchmen about the garden hoping to snare the Firebird, but it came no more for the golden apples.

Then Tsar Vyslav, greatly desiring it, sent for his two eldest sons and said: "Ye, my sons, failed even to see the thief of my apples, yet thy brother Ivan has at least brought me one of its feathers. Take horses now, with my blessing, and ride in search of it, and to the one of you who brings it to me alive I will give the half of my Tsardom." And Tsareviches Dimitry and Vasily, envious of their younger brother Ivan, rejoiced that their father did not bid him also go, and mounting their swift horses rode away gladly, both of them, in search of the Firebird.

They rode for three days—whether by a near or a far road, or on highland or lowland, the tale is soon told, but the journey is not done quickly—till they came to a green plain from whose centre three roads started, and there a great stone was set with these words carved upon it:

> Who rides straight forward shall know both hunger and cold.
> Who rides to the right shall live, though his steed shall be dead.
> Who rides to the left shall die, though his steed shall live.

They were uncertain which way to go, since none of the three roads promised well. At last they turned aside into a pleasant wood, pitched their silken tents and gave themselves over to rest and idle enjoyment.

Now when days had passed and they did not return, Tsarevich Ivan besought his father to give him also his blessing, with leave to ride forth to search for the Firebird, but Tsar Vyslav denied him, saying: "My dear son, the wolves will devour thee. Thou art still young and unused to far and difficult journeying. Enough that thy brothers have gone from me. I am already old in age and walk under the eye of God; if He take away my life, and thou, too, art gone, who will remain to keep order in my Tsardom? Rebellion may arise and there will be no one to quell it, or an enemy may cross our borders and there will be no one to command our troops. Seek not, therefore, to leave me!"

In spite of all, however, Tsarevich Ivan would not leave off his beseeching till at length his father consented, and he took Tsar Vyslav's blessing, chose a swift horse for his use and rode away he knew not whither.

Three days he rode, till he came to the green plain whence the three ways started and read the words carved on the great stone that stood there. "I may not take the left road, lest I die," he thought, "nor the middle road, lest I know hunger and cold. Rather will I take the right-hand road, whereon, though my poor horse perish, I at least shall keep my life." So he reined to the right.

He rode one day, he rode two days, he rode three days, and on the morning of the fourth day, as he led his horse through a forest, a great Grey Wolf leaped from a thicket. "Thou art a brave lad, Tsarevich Ivan," said the Wolf, "but didst thou not read what was written on the rock?" When the Wolf had spoken these words, he seized the horse and, tearing it in pieces, devoured it and disappeared.

Tsarevich Ivan wept bitterly over the loss of his horse. The whole day he walked, till his weariness could not be told in a tale. He was near to faint from weakness, when again he met the Grey Wolf. "Thou art a brave lad, Tsarevich Ivan," said the Wolf, "and for this reason I feel pity for thee. I have eaten thy good horse, but I will serve thee a service in payment. Sit now on my back and say whither I shall bear thee and wherefore."

Tsarevich Ivan seated himself on the back of the Wolf joyfully enough. "Take me, Grey Wolf," he said, "to the Firebird that stole my father's golden apples," and instantly the Wolf sped away, twenty times swifter than the swiftest horse. In the middle of the night he stopped at a stone wall.

"Get down from my back, Tsarevich Ivan," said the Wolf, "and climb over this wall. On the other side is a garden, and in the garden is an iron railing, and behind the railing three cages are hung, one of copper, one of silver, and one of gold. In the copper cage is a crow, in the silver one is a jackdaw, and in the golden cage is the Firebird. Open the door of the golden cage, take out the Firebird, and wrap it in thy handkerchief. But on no account take the golden cage; if thou dost, great misfortune will follow."

Tsarevich Ivan climbed the wall, entered the iron railing and found the three cages as the Grey Wolf had said. He took out the Firebird and wrapped it in his handkerchief, but he could not bear to leave behind him the beautiful golden cage.

The instant he stretched out his hand and took it, however, there sounded throughout all the garden a great noise of clanging bells and the twanging of musical instruments to which the golden cage was tied by many invisible cords, and fifty watchmen, waking, came running into the garden. They seized Tsarevich Ivan, and in the morning they brought him before their Tsar, who was called Dolmat.

Tsar Dolmat was greatly angered and shouted in a loud voice: "How now! This is a fine, bold handed Cossack to be caught in such a shameful theft! Who art thou, from what country comest thou? Of what father art thou son, and how art thou named?"

столба сего прям
и холоденъ
кто поѣдетъ въ
правую сторону
будетъ здравъ и жи
а конь мертвъ
а кто поѣдетъ
лѣвую сторону
самъ убитъ будетъ
конь живъ
И. БИЛИБИНЪ 1899

"I come from the Tsardom of Vyslav," answered Tsarevich Ivan, "son of Tsar Vyslav, and I am called Ivan. Thy Firebird entered my father's garden by night and stole many golden apples from his favourite tree. Therefore the Tsar, my father, sent me to find and bring to him the thief."

"And how should I know that thou speakest truth?" answered Tsar Dolmat. "Hadst thou come to me first, I would have given thee the Firebird with honour. How will it be with thee now when I send into all Tsardoms, declaring how thou hast acted shamefully in my borders? However, Tsarevich Ivan, I will excuse thee this if thou wilt serve me a certain service. If thou wilt ride across three times nine countries to the thirtieth Tsardom of Tsar Afron and wilt win for me from him the Horse with the Golden Mane, which his father promised me and which is mine by right, then will I give to thee with all joy the Firebird. But if thou dost not serve me this service, then will I declare throughout all Tsardoms that thou art a thief, unworthy to share thy father's honours."

Tsarevich Ivan went out from Tsar Dolmat in great grief. He found the Grey Wolf and related to him the whole.

"Thou art a foolish youth, Tsarevich Ivan," said the Wolf. "Why didst thou not recall my words and leave the golden cage?"

"I am guilty before thee!" answered Ivan sorrowfully.

"Well," said the Grey Wolf, "I will help thee. Sit on my back and say whither I shall bear thee and wherefore."

So Tsarevich Ivan a second time mounted the Wolf's back. "Take me, Grey Wolf," he said, "across three times nine countries to the thirtieth Tsardom, to Tsar Afron's Horse with the Golden Mane."

At once the Wolf began running, fifty times swifter than the swiftest horse. Whether it was a long way or a short way, in the middle of the night he came to the thirtieth Tsardom, to Tsar Afron's Palace, and stopped beside the royal stables, which were built all of white stone.

"Now, Tsarevich Ivan," said the Wolf, "get down from my back and open the door. The stablemen are all fast asleep, and thou mayest win the Horse with the Golden Mane. Only take not the golden bridle that hangs beside it. If thou takest that, great ill will befall thee."

Tsarevich Ivan opened the door of the stables, and there he saw the Horse with the Golden Mane, whose brightness was such that the whole stall was lighted by it. But as he was leading it out, he saw the golden bridle, and its beauty tempted him to take it also. Scarcely had he touched it, however, when there arose a great clanging and thundering, for the bridle was tied by many cords to instruments of brass. The noise awakened the stablemen, who came running, a hundred of them, and seized Tsarevich Ivan, and in the morning led him before Tsar Afron.

The Tsar was much surprised to see so gallant a youth accused of such a theft. "What!" he said. "Thou art a goodly lad to be a robber of my horses! Tell me: from what Tsardom dost thou come, son of what father art thou, and what is thy name?"

"I come from the Tsardom of Tsar Vyslav," replied Tsarevich Ivan, "whose son I am, and my name is Ivan. Tsar Dolmat laid upon me this service, that I bring him the Horse with the Golden Mane, which thy father promised him and which is his by right."

"Hadst thou come with such a word from Tsar Dolmat," answered Tsar Afron, "I would have given thee the horse with honour, and thou needst not have taken it from me by stealth. How will it be with thee when I send my heralds into all Tsardoms declaring thee, a Tsar's son, to be a thief? However, Tsarevich Ivan, I will excuse thee this if thou wilt serve me a certain service. Thou shalt ride over three times nine lands to the country of the Tsar whose daughter is known as Helen the Beautiful, and bring me the Tsarevna to be my wife. For I have loved her for long with my soul and my heart, and yet cannot win her. Do this, and I will forgive thee this fault and with joy will give thee the Horse with the Golden Mane and the golden bridle also for Tsar Dolmat. But if thou dost not serve me this service, then will I name thee as a shameful thief in all Tsardoms."

Tsarevich Ivan went out from the splendid Palace weeping many tears, came to the Grey Wolf and told him all that had befallen.

"Thou hast again been a foolish youth!" said the Wolf. "Why didst thou not remember my warning not to touch the golden bridle?"

"Grey Wolf," said Ivan still weeping, "I am guilty before thee!"

"Well," said the Wolf, "be it so. I will help thee. Sit upon my back and say whither I shall bear thee and wherefore."

So Tsarevich Ivan wiped away his tears and a third time mounted the Wolf's back. "Take me, Grey Wolf," he said, "across three times nine lands to the Tsarevna who is called Helen the Beautiful."

And straightway the Wolf began running, a hundred times swifter than the swiftest horse, faster than one can tell in a tale, until he came to the country of the beautiful princess. At length he stopped at a golden railing surrounding a lovely garden.

"Get down now, Tsarevich Ivan," said the Wolf, "go back along the road by which we came, and wait for me in the open field under the green oak tree." So Tsarevich Ivan did as he was bidden. But as for the Grey Wolf, he waited there.

Toward evening, when the sun was very low and its rays were no longer hot, the Tsar's daughter, Helen the Beautiful, went into the garden to walk with her nurse and the ladies-in-waiting of the Court. When she came near, suddenly the Grey Wolf leaped over the railing into the garden, seized her and ran off with her more swiftly than twenty horses. He ran to the open field, to the green oak tree, where Tsarevich Ivan was waiting, and set her down beside him. Helen the Beautiful had been greatly frightened but dried her tears quickly when she saw the handsome youth.

"Mount my back, Tsarevich Ivan," said the Wolf, "and take the Tsarevna in your arms."

Tsarevich Ivan sat on the Grey Wolf's back and took Helen the Beautiful in his arms, and the Wolf began running more swiftly than fifty horses, across the three times nine countries, back to the Tsardom of Tsar Afron. The nurse and ladies-in-waiting of the Tsarevna hastened to the Palace, and the Tsar sent many troops in pursuit, but fast as they went they could not overtake the Grey Wolf.

Sitting on the Wolf's back, with the Tsar's beautiful daughter in his arms, Tsarevich Ivan began to love her with his heart and soul, and Helen the Beautiful began also to love him, so that when the Grey Wolf came to the country of Tsar Afron, to whom she was to be given, Tsarevich Ivan began to shed many tears.

"Why dost thou weep, Tsarevich Ivan?" asked the Wolf, and Ivan answered: "Grey Wolf, my friend! Why should I not weep and be desolate? I myself have begun to love Helen the Beautiful, yet now I must give her up to Tsar Afron for the Horse with the Golden Mane. For if I do not, then Tsar Afron will dishonour my name in all countries."

"I have served thee in much, Tsarevich Ivan," said the Grey Wolf, "but I will also do thee this service. Listen: when we come near to the Palace, I myself will take the shape of the Tsar's daughter, and thou shalt lead me to Tsar Afron and shalt take in exchange the Horse with the Golden Mane. Thou shalt mount it and ride far away. Then I will ask leave of Tsar Afron to walk on the open steppe, and when I am on the steppe with the Court ladies-in-waiting, thou hast only to think of me, the Grey Wolf, and I shall come once more to thee."

As soon as the Wolf had uttered these words, he beat his paw against the damp ground and instantly took the shape of the Tsar's beautiful daughter: so like to her that no one in the world could have told that he was not the Tsarevna herself. Then, bidding Helen the Beautiful wait for him outside the walls, Tsarevich Ivan led the Grey Wolf into the Palace to Tsar Afron.

The Tsar, thinking at last he had won the treasure he had so long desired as his wife, was very joyful and gave Tsarevich Ivan, for Tsar Dolmat, the Horse with the Golden Mane and the golden bridle. And Tsarevich Ivan, mounting, rode outside the walls to the real Helen the Beautiful, put her before him on the saddle and set out across the three times nine countries back to the Tsardom of Tsar Dolmat.

As to the Grey Wolf, he spent one day, he spent two days, he spent three days in Tsar Afron's Palace, all the while having the shape of the beautiful Tsarevna, while the Tsar made preparations for a splendid bridal. On the fourth day he asked the Tsar's permission to go for a walk on the open steppe.

"Oh, my beautiful Tsar's daughter," said Tsar Afron, "I grant thee whatever thou mayest wish. Go then and walk where it pleaseth thee, and perchance it will soothe thy grief and sorrow at parting from thy father." So he ordered serving-women and all the ladies-in-waiting of the Court to walk with her.

But all at once, as they walked on the open steppe, Tsarevich Ivan, far away, riding with the real Helen the Beautiful on the Horse with the Golden Mane, suddenly bethought himself and cried: "Grey Wolf, Grey Wolf, I am thinking of thee now! Where art thou?" At that very instant the false Princess, as she walked with the ladies-in-waiting of Tsar Afron's Court, turned into the Grey Wolf, which ran off more swiftly than seventy horses. The ladies-in-waiting hastened to the Palace, and Tsar Afron sent many soldiers in pursuit, but they could not catch the Grey Wolf, and soon he overtook Tsarevich Ivan.

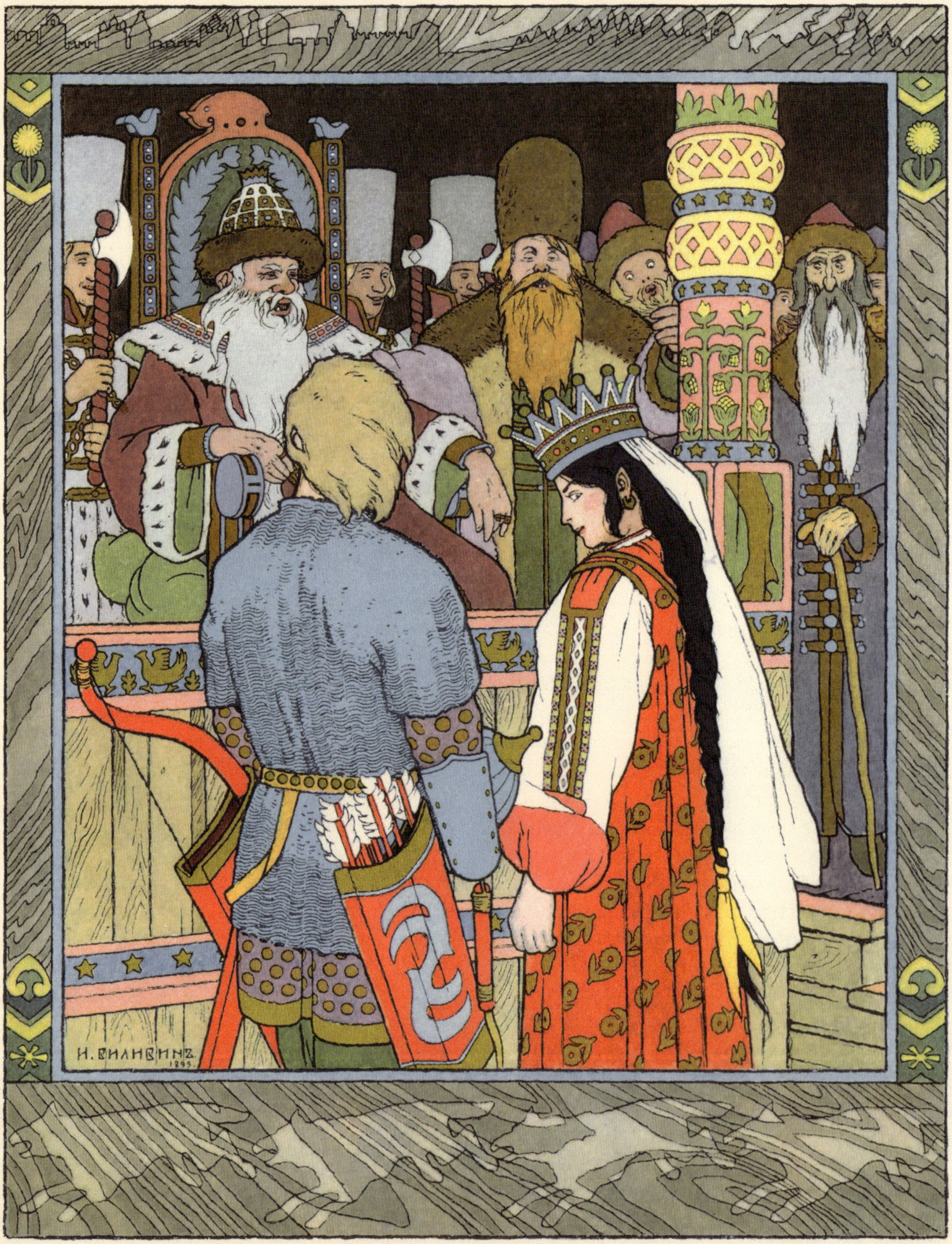
И. БИЛИБИНЪ.
1899.

"Mount on my back, Tsarevich Ivan," said the Wolf, "and let Helen the Beautiful ride on the Horse with the Golden Mane."

Tsarevich Ivan mounted the Grey Wolf, and the Tsarevna rode on the Horse with the Golden Mane, and so they went on together to the Tsardom of Tsar Dolmat, in whose garden hung the cage with the Firebird. Whether the way was a long one or a short one, at length they came near to Tsar Dolmat's Palace. Then Tsarevich Ivan, getting down from the Wolf's back, said:

"Grey Wolf, my dear friend! Thou hast served me many services. Serve me also one more, the last and greatest. If thou canst take the shape of Helen the Beautiful, thou canst take also that of the Horse with the Golden Mane. Do this and let me deliver thee to Tsar Dolmat in exchange for the Firebird. Then, when I am far away on the road to my own Tsardom, thou canst again rejoin us."

"So be it," said the Wolf and beat his paw against the dry ground, and immediately he took the shape of the Horse with the Golden Mane, so like to that the Princess rode that no one could have told one from the other. Then Tsarevich Ivan, leaving Helen the Beautiful on the green lawn with the real Horse with the Golden Mane, mounted and rode to the Palace gate.

When Tsar Dolmat saw Tsarevich Ivan riding on the false Horse with the Golden Mane, he rejoiced exceedingly. He came out, embraced Ivan in the wide courtyard and kissed him on the mouth, and taking his right hand, led him into his splendid rooms. He made a great festival, and they sat at oak tables covered with embroidered cloths and for two days ate, drank and made merry.

On the third day the Tsar gave to Tsarevich Ivan the Firebird in its golden cage. Ivan took it, went to the green lawn where he had left Helen the Beautiful, mounted the real Horse with the Golden Mane, set the Tsarevna on the saddle before him, and together they rode away across the three times nine lands towards his native country, the Tsardom of Tsar Vyslav.

As to Tsar Dolmat, for two days he admired the false Horse with the Golden Mane, and on the third day he desired to ride it. He gave orders, therefore, to saddle it and, mounting, rode to the open steppe. But as he was riding, it chanced that Tsarevich Ivan, far away with Helen the Beautiful, all at once remembered his promise and cried: "Grey Wolf, Grey Wolf, I am thinking of thee!" And at that instant the horse Tsar Dolmat rode threw him from its back and turned into the Grey Wolf, which ran off more swiftly than a hundred horses.

Tsar Dolmat hastened to the Palace and sent many soldiers in pursuit, but they could not catch the Grey Wolf, who soon overtook the Horse with the Golden Mane that bore Tsarevich Ivan and the Tsarevna.

"Get down, Tsarevich Ivan," said the Wolf, "mount my back and let Helen the Beautiful ride on the Horse with the Golden Mane."

So Tsarevich Ivan mounted the Grey Wolf, and the Tsarevna rode on the Horse with the Golden Mane, and at length they came to the forest where the Wolf had devoured Tsarevich Ivan's horse.

There the Grey Wolf stopped. "Well, Tsarevich Ivan," he said, "I have paid for thy horse and have served thee in faith and truth. Get down now; I am no longer thy servant."

Tsarevich Ivan got down from the Wolf's back, weeping many tears that they should part, and the Grey Wolf leaped into a thicket and disappeared, leaving Tsarevich Ivan, mounted on the Horse with the Golden Mane, with Helen the Beautiful in his arms who held in her hands the golden cage in which was the Firebird, to ride to the Palace of Tsar Vyslav.

They rode on three days, till they came to the green plain where the three ways met and where stood the great stone, and being very tired the Tsarevich and the Tsarevna here dismounted and lay down to rest. They tied the Horse with the Golden Mane to the stone, and lying lovingly side by side on the soft grass, they went to sleep.

Now it happened that the two elder brothers of Ivan, Tsarevich Dimitry and Tsarevich Vasily, having tired of their amusements in the wood and being minded to return to their father without the Firebird, came riding past the spot and found their brother lying asleep with Helen the Beautiful beside him. Seeing not only that he had found the Firebird, but a horse with a mane of gold and a lovely Princess, they were envious, and Tsarevich Dimitry drew his sword, stabbed Tsarevich Ivan to death, and cut his body into small pieces. They then awoke Helen the Beautiful and began to question her.

"Lovely stranger," they asked, "from what Tsardom dost thou come, of what father art thou daughter, and how art thou named?"

Helen the Beautiful, being roughly awakened and seeing Tsarevich Ivan dead, was greatly frightened and cried with bitter tears: "I am the Tsar's daughter, Helen the Beautiful, and I belong to Tsarevich Ivan whom ye have put to a cruel death. If ye were brave knights, ye had ridden against him in the open field; then might ye have been victorious over him with honour; but instead of that ye have slain him when he was asleep! What praise will such an act receive?"

But Tsarevich Vasily set the point of his sword against her breast and said: "Listen, Helen the Beautiful! Thou art now in our hands. We shall bring thee to our father, Tsar Vyslav, and thou shalt tell him that we, and not Tsarevich Ivan, found the Firebird and won the Horse with the Golden Mane and thine own lovely self. If thou dost not swear by all holy things to say this, then this instant will we put thee to death!" And the beautiful Tsar's daughter, frightened by their threats, swore that she would speak as they commanded.

Tsarevich Dimitry and Tsarevich Vasily cast lots to see who should take Helen the Beautiful and who the Horse with the Golden Mane and the Firebird. The Princess fell to Tsarevich Vasily and the horse and the bird to Tsarevich Dimitry. So Tsarevich Vasily took Helen the Beautiful on his horse, and Tsarevich Dimitry took the Firebird and the Horse with the Golden Mane, and both rode swiftly to the Palace of their father, Tsar Vyslav.

The Tsar rejoiced greatly to see them. To Tsarevich Dimitry, since he had brought him the Firebird, he gave the half of his Tsardom, and he made a festival which lasted a whole month, at the end of which time Tsarevich Vasily was to wed the Princess, Helen the Beautiful.

As for Tsarevich Ivan, dead and cut into pieces, he lay on the green plain for thirty days. And on the thirty first day it chanced that the Grey Wolf passed that way. He knew at once by his keen scent that the body was that of Tsarevich Ivan. While he sat grieving for his friend, there came flying an iron-beaked she-crow with two fledglings, who alighted on the ground and would have eaten of the flesh, but the Wolf leaped up and seized one of the young birds.

Then the mother Crow, flying to a little distance, said to him: "O Grey Wolf, wolf's son! Do not devour my little child, since it has in no way harmed thee!"

And the Grey Wolf answered: "Listen, Crow, crow's daughter! Serve me a certain service, and I will not harm thy fledgling. I have heard that across three times nine countries, in the thirtieth Tsardom, are two springs, so placed that none save a bird can come to them, which give forth, the one the water of death, and the other the water of life. Bring to me two bottles of these waters, and I will let thy fledgling go safe and sound. But if thou dost not, then I will tear it into pieces and devour it."

"I will indeed do thee this service, Grey Wolf, wolf's son," said the Crow, "only harm not my child," and immediately flew away as swiftly as an arrow.

The Grey Wolf waited one day, he waited two days, he waited three days, and on the fourth day the she-crow came flying with two little bottles of water in her beak.

The Grey Wolf tore the fledgling into pieces and sprinkled the pieces with the water of death, and they instantly grew together; he sprinkled the dead body with the water of life, and the fledgling shook itself and flew away with the she-crow, safe and sound. The Grey Wolf then sprinkled the pieces of the body of Tsarevich Ivan with the water of death, and they grew together; he sprinkled the dead body with the water of life, and Tsarevich Ivan stood up, stretched himself and said: "How long I must have slept!"

"Yes, Tsarevich Ivan," the Grey Wolf said, "and thou wouldst have slept forever had it not been for me. For thy brothers cut thee into pieces and took away with them the beautiful Tsar's daughter, the Horse with the Golden Mane and the Firebird. Make haste now and mount on my back, for thy brother Tsarevich Vasily today is to wed thy Helen the Beautiful."

Tsarevich Ivan made haste to mount, and the Grey Wolf began running, swifter than a hundred horses, toward the Palace of Tsar Vyslav.

Whether the way was long or short, he came soon to the city, and there at the gate the Grey Wolf stopped. "Get down now, Tsarevich Ivan," he said. "I am no longer a servant of thine, and thou shalt see me no more, but sometimes remember the journeys thou hast made on the back of the Grey Wolf."

Tsarevich Ivan got down and, having bade the Wolf farewell with tears, entered the city and went at once to the Palace, where Tsarevich Vasily was even then being wed to Helen the Beautiful.

He entered the splendid rooms and came where they sat at table, and as soon as Helen the Beautiful saw him, she sprang up from the table and kissed him on the mouth, crying: "This is my beloved, Tsarevich Ivan, who shall wed me, and not this wicked one, Tsarevich Vasily, who sits with me at table!"

Tsar Vyslav rose up in his place and questioned Helen the Beautiful, and she related to him the whole: how Tsarevich Ivan had won her with the Horse with the Golden Mane and the Firebird, and how his two elder brothers had slain him as he lay asleep and had threatened her with death so that she should say what they bade.

Tsar Vyslav, hearing, was angered like a great river in a storm. He commanded that Tsareviches Dimitry and Vasily be seized and thrown into prison, and Tsarevich Ivan, that same day, was wed to Helen the Beautiful. The Tsar made a great feast, and all the people drank wine and mead till it ran down their beards, and the festival lasted many days till there was no one hungry or thirsty in the whole Tsardom.

And when the rejoicing was over, the two elder brothers were made, one a scullion and the other a cowherd, but Tsarevich Ivan lived always with Helen the Beautiful in such harmony and love that neither of them could bear to be without the other even for a single moment.

Printed in Great Britain
by Amazon